SOLO VIOLA

A UNIVOCAL BOOK
Drew Burk, Consulting Editor

Univocal Publishing was founded by Jason Wagner and Drew Burk as an independent publishing house specializing in artisanal editions and translations of texts spanning the areas of cultural theory, media archaeology, continental philosophy, aesthetics, anthropology, and more. In May 2017, Univocal ceased operations as an independent publishing house and became a series with its publishing partner the University of Minnesota Press.

Univocal authors include:

Miguel Abensour	Évelyne Grossman	Jacques Rancière
Judith Balso	Félix Guattari	Lionel Ruffel
Jean Baudrillard	David Lapoujade	Felwine Sarr
Philippe Beck	François Laruelle	Michel Serres
Simon Critchley	David Link	Gilbert Simondon
Fernand Deligny	Sylvère Lotringer	Étienne Souriau
Jacques Derrida	Jean Malaurie	Isabelle Stengers
Vinciane Despret	Michael Marder	Eugene Thacker
Georges Didi-Huberman	Serge Margel	Antoine Volodine
Jean Epstein	Quentin Meillassoux	Elisabeth von Samsonow
Vilém Flusser	Friedrich Nietzsche	Siegfried Zielinski
Barbara Glowczewski	Peter Pál Pelbart	

SOLO VIOLA

A POST-EXOTIC NOVEL

Antoine Volodine

Translated by Lia Swope Mitchell

A UNIVOCAL BOOK

University of Minnesota Press
Minneapolis
London

This work received support from the French Ministry of Foreign Affairs and the Cultural Services of the French Embassy in the United States through their publishing program.

Originally published in French as *Alto Solo,* copyright Les Éditions de Minuit, 1991.

Published by the University of Minnesota Press
111 Third Avenue South, Suite 290
Minneapolis, MN 55401-2520
http://www.upress.umn.edu

ISBN 978-1-5179-1119-5
A Cataloging-in-Publication record for this book is available from the Library of Congress.

Printed in the United States of America on acid-free paper

The University of Minnesota is an equal-opportunity educator and employer.

29 28 27 26 25 24 23 22 21   10 9 8 7 6 5 4 3 2 1

CONTENTS ·

.

FOREWORD · LIONEL RUFFEL

AS I BEGIN WRITING THIS FOREWORD, I find myself wondering what path to take.

I think of you, the reader; I imagine you as a reader of literature, probably not a French speaker, but curious, and open to what is often poorly named "foreign literature"—and even more poorly named in this case, since the author of the book you've opened once made the oft-cited statement that he was writing "a foreign literature in French."[1]

So you're holding this book in your hands, and the illusion is perfect: on the cover, you read what looks like an author's name: Antoine Volodine; and the title of the work: *Solo Viola*. We could, and perhaps we should, leave it at that: nothing but the book you hold in your hands. Especially since, thirty years after its first publication, this book has never seemed more current.

No doubt, one characteristic (perhaps a curse?) of Volodine's work is that it is constantly made current again by a world that it holds at a distance. One might almost say that the author is like one of the characters in *Solo Viola*, the writer whose portrait you will read further on: "When he can find nothing good about the world from any perspective, the writer, Iakoub Khadjbakiro, takes his paper and transforms the fabric of truth. He is not content to offer peevish, bitter pronouncements about the world that surrounds him. He does not reproduce in exact detail the elemental brutality to which humanity has been reduced, the bestial tragedy of their fate."

Reading this book first published in 1991, you may feel as if you were emerging "from the subterranean levels of mirage," onto "the main square" of many capital cities in 2021, on both sides of the Atlantic and all around the world. We are in Washington, D.C., in Brasília, in Manila, London, Pyongyang, Paris, Ashgabat—we are everywhere, today or tomorrow, even more than yesterday. Of course, we can and even must recognize Balynt Zagoebel (the tyrant of Chamrouche, the invented city where *Solo Viola* is set) as an altered image of the dictatorships of the previous century, the Nazis first among them; but most of all, we can recognize the image of the "malevolent buffoons"[2] who have come to dominate the political world.

For the most part, although not exclusively, this is how the book was read when it appeared in France, when Jean-Marie Le Pen, a forefather of our contemporary "malevolent buffoons," was leading his party to its first electoral successes. But all of it was only potential; not until the beginning of the twenty-first century did this nightmare really begin to take shape. Balynt Zagoebel's "rally-spectacular" anticipates the racist entertainment-politics of the current occupants in high offices the whole world over: it's an event where, "through their ears, their eyes, their every pore, the crowd could slake both its thirst for entertainment and the desire for condemnation."

Rereading *Solo Viola* in 2020, as I am doing today, produces a strange sensation of discovering our world as it was anticipated thirty years ago, by a writer who, like his character, worked "to replace the hideousness of current events with his own absurd images. His own partial hallucinations, both troubled and troubling." As if the world has finally caught up to that absurdity.

You might ask me: Why bother reading a fictional work, if reality seems to have caught up with it? There are many reasons, both literary and historical, political and philosophical, and I will return to them; but on the historical and political side, let us keep in mind that, in *Solo Viola,* the tyranny of malevolent buffoons is not exercised only on the level of race but also on the level of species.

"NO NEGS AND NO SPADGERS WILL BE SERVED IN THIS ESTABLISHMENT," we read, posted in a café. And in fact, at least one of the characters in this book (I will say no more, so as to maintain the suspense) is a "spadger": a bird who is quite clearly persecuted, along with other members of his species. The murderous racism of the malevolent buffoon and his henchmen is primarily, although not exclusively (it also falls on "negs" and artists), exerted against birds, even if they are not really distinguishable from humans, and humans not really distinguishable from birds. A few feathers here, a beak over there, no more. Antoine Volodine is one of the first contemporary authors whose body of work takes the porousness of interspecies boundaries, and consequently the new political battles about how to erect those boundaries, as one of its foundational aspects.

Volodine named a main character Ingrid Vogel ("Vogel" means "bird" in German) as early as 1990 (that is, one year before *Solo Viola*, and after four books published in a science fiction series), in *Lisbon, dernier marge*, his first novel within the field of consecrated literature, published by the prestigious Éditions de Minuit. From his earliest works and up until today, animals abound in Volodine's books—especially animals that live in packs and groups—and they hybridize human space.

I remember how much this element surprised and even bothered me when I began to read Volodine's work. I did not understand it. I was interested, I was intrigued, but I did not understand it. Now that no one can claim ignorance of the sixth extinction, the climate crisis, or the effects of what some call the Anthropocene—although, really, we need a whole range of names, like Capitalocene, Plantationocene, Chthulucene—Volodine's books from the 1990s can be read differently: they are regenerated by this extension of politics across the whole spectrum of the living. Over the past few years, we have received confirmation of what Volodine already imagined in *Solo Viola*: the malevolent buffoon, in his thirst for destruction, erects the same boundaries in the conception of the living as he does around the conception of humanity. Faced with this politics of terror, an "immigrant composer" mentioned in the book takes a heartrending stance. Before his suicide, he pins onto his sweater "this very explicit request: I beg you, do not bury me with representatives of the human race."

But of course, we don't read novels to learn a political lesson, even if the lesson is always coming. And from this perspective, (re)reading *Solo Viola* is first and foremost an encounter with a narrative jewel in its raw, pure state. The structure is tragic—respecting the unities of time, space, and action—at least in the first two parts, which take place on May 27 (you may wish to search on your own for any events that took place on some May 27 in the twentieth century; Volodine's narrations often continue the revolutionary custom of paying tribute through dates); the much shorter third part takes place a month later. The first two parts, the "Afternoon of May 27" and "Evening of May 27," are models of variation and narrative pertinence.

The very cinematic first part uses the phrase "This is the story of" to multiply its approaches and viewpoints, endlessly refining and correcting. Although its goal is to set the scene of a rich fictional world, the capital of an imaginary country, with a multitude of characters and situations, this first part is also playful, correcting itself, varying its perspectives, superimposing them. Things and beings appear to us and then transform before our eyes; at once brilliant and powerful, this part reminds us that fiction reigns supreme, and there is no need to make a choice between *telling,* or finding a form, and *story,* or transmitting a plot. Volodine *tells a story* and carries us along with this virtuosic beginning, into the world of the tale, one that does not hide its artifice but never fails to hold our attention.

In the second part, we change perspective. Whereas the variations that compose the first section gave an impression of lightness, the second part is presented entirely as a single narrative block, with an increasingly perceptible slow-motion effect that takes on the inevitability of approaching disaster. The narrator tries to push that disaster away as much as possible, without success. There is also a third part, but a foreword must not say too much.

For professional reasons as well as taste, I spend a great deal of my life reading literary works. There are so many good authors that I can't see any reason to read mediocre ones. But there are also extraordinary authors, and a single phrase is enough to alert us to the fact that we've changed categories. The opening of *Solo Viola* is an example: "This is the story of a man. Of two men. Actually, three." It is perfect and lends a literary tone to the text that follows, which you are about to discover.

But before you plunge into reading, I'd like to come back to that overly quick assertion I mentioned earlier: that you'll be reading a book titled *Solo Viola,* by an author named Antoine Volodine. This information is only partially true, but most of all, it is incomplete. One day, in a lecture given at the Bibliothèque Nationale de France, the man who calls himself Antoine Volodine spoke on the topic of this signature and this constantly evolving body of work. Here is what he said:

> One must see and understand Antoine Volodine as a collective signature that undertakes the writings, voices, and poems of several other authors. One must understand my physical presence, before this microphone, as the presence of a delegate whose task is to represent the others, my comrades who have been prevented from appearing before you due to their mental distance, their incarceration, or their death. One must allow my presence here as a spokesman. A spokesman for post-exoticism, an imaginary literature, coming from elsewhere and going elsewhere, a literature that proudly claims its status as foreign and strange, that proudly claims its singularity, and that refuses any attribution to a specific and clearly identifiable national literature.[3]

You can read *Solo Viola* without any awareness that the place of this short novel is not just within a body of work; rather, it emerges as part of a corpus or a library, along with the very name Antoine Volodine, as well as Lutz Bassmann, Elli Kronauer, or Manuela Draeger, heteronyms of this author-turned-collective. Even better, you can read *Solo Viola* as you might read a tale from the *One Thousand and One Nights*: for the individual pleasure that it brings you, but also because it exists within a frame narrative, in which a narrator, a prisoner, resists death by telling stories. Post-exoticism, as this literature is called, forms that frame narrative. Sometimes it is explicitly mentioned in the texts, but more often it is left implicit, giving these works a supplement of meaning that carries us elsewhere, toward an even more powerful experience than reading, an experience that Volodine describes as magical or shamanic. In this frame narrative, political activists, militants of radical egalitarianism, are imprisoned, nearly or already dead, and are trying to communicate amongst themselves, as if with their last breath—trying to give new form to the beauties and disasters of an already ended world. This power of narration to trick death, this feeling that the end is imminent or already in the past—isn't this the feeling we have all been experiencing so profoundly in recent days, on a planetary scale? Post-exotic literature offers a hallucinatory version: the one thousand and one nights of our time.

Solo Viola may be your first entry into this world. Be advised, it is at once immense and finite; Volodine has stated that it will include forty-nine works. *Kree,* published in 2020 under the name Manuela Draeger, is the forty-fourth. If you begin here, with *Solo Viola,* in 2021, you may have time to read everything before the final book appears.

Translation by Lia Swope Mitchell

Notes

1. Antoine Volodine, "Écrire en français une littérature étrangère," *Chaoïd 6* (Autumn-Winter, 2002).

2. Christian Salmon, "La tyrannie des bouffons," *Mediapart*, June 14, 2020, https://www.mediapart.fr/journal/international/140620/la-tyrannie-des-bouffons.

3. Quoted in Michel Butor et al., *Neuf leçons de littérature* (Paris: Thierry Magnier, 2007), 151.

SOLO VIOLA

THIS IS THE STORY OF A MAN. Of two men. Actually, three. Aram, Matko, and Will MacGrodno. The prison door closes behind them. It slams. The iron hinges bang together. They produce the same thunder as always, like train cars suddenly derailing and crashing into each other. The same deafening racket as always. And yet there's a difference. Today, as the three men listen to those echoes die out, they're not standing in the prison's corridors, in its stairwells, or under its skylights, but instead, out in the warm street. High walls loom over them, every bit as forbidding as the ones that, for the past four years, formed the boundaries of their world. But now, on this familiar cement, no bars fence off the sun. A truck snorts across the nearby intersection and disappears. The three men can feel dust filling their nostrils, the change in the air's consistency. Truly, now, they have ceased to swim in the lingering stench of toilets and rags. They don't know quite what to think. Just before the guard set off the racket, the oily avalanche of locks and ratchets and bars, he tossed them a sort of farewell: That's enough, nobody wants you here. We're sick of your dirty faces. Find some other castle to call home. Go get hanged somewhere else!

They have no clear understanding of what's just happened. Early release, for lack of space rather than good behavior. An order from the minister of Justice. Somewhere on high, someone must have foreseen a new batch of clients. Conditional release, with eighteen months' probation. The prison's kicked them out, more or less, but threatens to take them back for the slightest false move. Before leaving the three men signed, without enthusiasm, a large black register. Their names appeared in alphabetical order: Amirbekian, Bouderbichvili, MacGrodno. Now, dazed in the sunlight, they drift forward. After five or six meters, they come to rest on the sidewalk. If they had a cigarette, they'd light it and pass it between them. But they have no cigarette. Their entire fortune amounts to fifteen cents: eight cents for Aram, six cents for Matko Amirbekian, one cent for Will MacGrodno. A tiny stream twists through the gutter. A swelling vein beneath a crumbly layer of clay. They watch the water creep along. They observe it snaking uncertainly past their feet, picking up bristly bits of sawdust. Sitting on the ground with their hands on their knees and their heads bent, they look like three nursing-home patients, the kind who piss themselves and then stare for hours at their soaked slippers. As if meditating.

Behind them the locks and hinges produce another infernal racket. The guard's been spying on them through the window. He takes the trouble to stick his helmet out into the street and yells: Look, guys, you can't set up camp out here! Then a rough, fatherly tone softens his voice. Come on, guys, say a prayer for the past and get moving! You've still got your whole lives ahead of you. Here's hoping we never meet again!

So the three men get up. They angle toward a deserted street. Two hundred meters down, they sit on an asphalt ledge in front of a saw-mill, where the machines have fallen quiet during the noon break. There, the three men count their change, fifteen cents total. They divide the coins into three equal shares and pocket them.

This is also the story of a bird. A bird who was unable to accompany his flock when they went south in the fall, due to a wing injury sustained during a brawl with the Frondists. He's taken refuge in an attic, under the mansard roof of a house slated for demolition, but not yet fallen under the axe. Through the broken windows, through the soot and cracks in the transom, he can see the street. The neighborhood is full of retired people, old women especially. Old women in mourning.

The bird's name is Ragojine. He suffers in this precarious, clandestine life that he leads, his solitary confinement in this cold, dilapidated house. He suffers, too, from the night's sudden screams: a bedlam of exploding windows and attacks, of hateful, roaring crowds. Solitude crushes him. He doesn't know anyone safe in Chamrouche, any other birds. Still other pains have taken root throughout his body. His injury was a bad one. The wound never healed and now it's festering, becoming infected. Scar tissue begins to form but soon enough the wound tears open again. Not even a single feather remains on his right side. Concentric marbling spreads across his necrotic skin. He hides his weakness and his fevers, he hides his avian nature under an overlarge raincoat, belted with a piece of string.

The black widows in the street have noticed him. They tolerate him. They have not betrayed him to the police, nor to the Party's hygiene patrols. Their pity stops there. At that negation of his existence. It never occurs to them to leave, for example, a pitcher of milk or a crust of bread on his doorstep. Ragojine must venture outside the neighborhood to find food. When he walks along the sidewalks, the people passing by turn to look. They size him up with damp, disdainful pouts. Their saliva foams with the desire to tear into him. In his effort to provoke them as little as possible, Ragojine doesn't allow his gaze to cross theirs. His eyes sweep the space that glitters just in front of his shoes. His large pupils carry neither plea nor insult. They express nothing. Their sole function is to capture images of cigarette butts, of edible garbage, of obstacles, human and otherwise. This way he hopes to avoid incidents, to avoid attracting any curiosity from the authorities, from veterans, from gangs. He has only slight experience of the capital, and he endures it like a long nightmare. He carries an absurd, childishly forged false passport. Fortunately, he's never had to show it to a patrol.

Huddled in Chamrouche, behind the cracked windows and spiderwebs, he tries to reach his flock through his dreams. He imagines he will manage to make contact while sleeping. So far, his vertiginous dozing has gotten him nowhere.

A bird, then, but in fact, this is the story of two birds. In the late '8os, Will MacGrodno was a member of Ragojine's flock. Just before his incarceration for arms trafficking and identity theft, Will MacGrodno lost his feathers. The guards didn't spare him any disciplinary drudgework on account of that. In his underground cell he sank into depression. But nothing could prevent him from staying true to himself. Despite the bars, despite the humiliations, he never stopped thinking of his people. Sometimes at night, he would visit a colony of birds wheeling over a blue landscape where they lived in grottoes at high altitude, in the hollow of a blue cliff, near a blue volcano whose smoke blanketed still valleys and plains of blue brush. These birds spoke a harsh dialect and considered him with visible hostility, like a lowborn relative. Will MacGrodno tossed on his cot. He woke. Sweat trickled across his downy torso. Beyond the bars, the moon shone. Dreams distill their relief only drop by drop.

In any case, on this twenty-seventh of May, Ragojine wanders around by the docks, between the marketplace and the port. It's one o'clock in the afternoon and the morning hubbub has stilled. The cleaning teams haven't gotten to work yet, the sellers in the market are done taking down their displays. The fishermen are eating lunch or dozing in their boats. There's some fruit lying around over here, some fish over there. Seagulls are pecking around farther off, in the sunshine. Ragojine crouches, stretches an emaciated hand toward the ground. He grabs a forgotten sardine lying next to an empty crate. On the damp asphalt, glittering in the light, the scales flash, the fins curve in red lines.

This is also the story of a clown. The story of a clown who works in the Vanzetti Circus, who has developed a phobia about everything related to death. There's nothing strange about that, but he's ashamed and strives to make sure nobody will notice. He doesn't want anyone to assume that his fear reveals some sort of weak or timorous character. Actually, his life is an extraordinary exercise in courage. His battle against fear structures every day of his life. He is a man bound to the circus, and yet the circus is a world where death is ever blooming—between the unpredictable fangs of beasts, on the tightrope where the funambulists defy the abyss, in the roll of the snare drum, which so clearly recalls the music that accompanies the firing squad when a deserter stands before them. Death infiltrates everything, it thrives there; it nests in the muddy, moldy atmosphere under the big top, it wafts in the lions' rotten-meat stench. And, of course, death ferments under the cackles of clowns, when, in order to unleash the audience's glee, they're forced to sacrifice some other clown.

This is the story, then, of a man devoured by a constant, incurable fear, but a man who prevails over that fear at every turn, as from that fear he earns his living. In the center ring, under the violent brilliance of the spotlights, he makes everyone laugh, young and old alike. He trips and falls before his colleague, who threatens him with a giant cardboard axe. He twirls and dashes in comical figure eights, crashing over the stools from the tiger act, stumbling with every step, surrounded by mouths that shout, bellies convulsed with laughter. Behind him an executioner bellows and scampers after him in oversized shoes. The victim does a perfect imitation of panic.

This clown's name is Baxir, and his stage name, on the Vanzetti Circus posters, is Kodek. Baxir Kodek the clown, who sobs with terror under the axe, under the laughter.

And already these many stories are becoming one. For a long time Baxir Kodek shared his trailer with another carny, a single man like himself. A friend, a confidant, a circus man, but this Bouderbichvili was almost impervious to fear. He was an accomplice as well. On moonless nights, after the show, after Vanzetti had finished his rounds and turned off the hurricane lamps marking the boundaries of the menagerie, Bouderbichvili and the clown would slip away, outside the poorly lit circle of their encampment. Together they stole across dark landscapes and trash heaps, into sleepy neighborhoods, into streets smothering under dim silence. They took advantage of broken streetlights. On utility poles, bus stops, and telephone booths, they pasted signs that summarized in a few words their opinions of the Party, the hygiene patrols, Frondism in general, and its leaders in particular. They disguised their writing so that the few people who read these texts would see little more than the scribbles of badly behaved children. Only Sarvara Dradjia the dwarf, a very dear friend to Baxir Kodek, ever discovered the two men's secret.

Bouderbichvili's act consisted of lifting iron weights or freestyle wrestling with volunteers from the audience. These adversaries, goaded by the audience or their own vicious instincts, assumed that any and all moves were permitted; this presented some delicate problems for the wrestler, who had to dominate his opponents without damaging them. One day, a huge muscle-bound Frondist—one of the giants working security for some Party big shot—came swaggering onto the mat. When the poorly positioned Frondist attempted a groin grab, Bouderbichvili accidentally crushed his neck under an awkward elbow. The right side of the Frondist's body was permanently paralyzed, left unfit for swaggering. The accident made the front page of the evening papers. Showing little leniency, the court sentenced Bouderbichvili to six years in the central prison of Chamrouche. The Vanzetti Circus was found culpable as well. To this day the circus pays heavy fines, emptying its budget into the Party's solidarity fund month after month.

Aram is the name of this unfortunate wrestler. Aram Bouderbichvili, who publicly humiliates Frondism's best henchmen.

This is also the story of a cellist. A cellist and a viola player. A man and a woman, but actually, they're four. Four young adults, none of them over thirty. After graduating from the Conservatory they formed a quartet, the Djylas Quartet. A quartet leading an unsettled, difficult life, dedicated to music. They're on the threshold of a promising career, but they're just starting out, and, regardless of their ability, they'll have to wait several years before critics recognize their true value. Since none of them has connections in political circles sympathetic to the Party or its followers, their path to success will be even longer. They've already found an audience, though, and they aren't playing to empty rooms. They play tours throughout the country's many provinces and even in foreign countries when international tensions permit, when the allied capitals are not at war against the South.

The viola player, Tchaki Estherkhan, is a girl with no particular physical grace, with chestnut hair in a hard frame around her features. She's big-boned, with somewhat heavy hips. Nevertheless, she is a girl, and the three male musicians of the quartet are in love with her. They court her, and sometimes, doing no damage to the harmony or cohesion of the group, she grants her favors to one or the other. In addition to the promiscuity of travel, which whips up the blood and incites debauchery, her musical talents are key to her romantic success. From her viola, she draws forth wondrous sounds. The technical level of the quartet is high, but Tchaki Estherkhan plays with unparalleled assurance, far better than her colleagues. One day, the cellist will listen to her and kill himself.

At the end of their concerts, when the listeners applauded and called for an encore, the two violinists and the cellist would fall back, and Tchaki Estherkhan alone would step forward, toward the audience. She performed pieces that she had adapted herself, transcriptions of Kaanto Djylas, the quartet's namesake composer, works by Danylo Tagrakian, Sevasti Palataï, Naïsso Baldakchan: their

most wrenching works, the ones written in exile. So enthralling was
the virtuosity she displayed that, as the audience listened, with their
breath caught and their eyes filling with sudden tears, few could believe that only a single instrument sang before them, that only four
strings vibrated for them. Tchaki Estherkhan created a sonic sphere
around herself, a harmonic richness surpassing the limits of human
understanding and memory. In these moments of enormous emotion, the walls fell away; the theater floated, wandered.

The theater would darken. Dimirtchi Makionian, the cellist,
would lean back in his uncomfortable chair, closing his eyes halfway.
Without dazzling footlights to blur her silhouette, Tchaki Estherkhan became the center of an abstract, starry landscape. She wore
a very simple black skirt, a plain blouse. She did not overdo the
vibrato. Nothing superfluous tainted her movements. Her austere
appearance banished any hint of spectacle, helping to open the way
into the miraculous heart of the music. Dimirtchi Makionian tried
to convince himself that the viola was addressed to him, exclusively
to him, and that Tchaki Estherkhan drew her magical inspiration
from the memory of a few tender nights they'd spent together. The
violinists, in their turn, bit their lips, trying to hide their exaltation
and emotion. They believed themselves the recipients of these
love letters, these chromatic flames, these cadences—plagal and
otherwise—of this flight.

But Tchaki Estherkhan was not thinking of her comrades and
colleagues, those three men sitting behind her and adoring her re-

ligiously, not even for a second. She drew no inspiration from what linked them, other than music, that friendly existence from which they too reverently extracted a few hours of abandon, voluptuous nights in hotel rooms, fleeting pleasures in sleeping cars. Bow in hand, she soared into strange and untethered worlds. And there she found a bird she had known before the formation of the quartet, before the tours, the contracts, the nomadic life. She met him while she was studying at the Conservatory, and loved him. The bird was weighted down with a funny name: Kirghyl Karakassian. After one summer of passion, he disappeared. Tchaki Estherkhan had not heard a single word from him since. But she could not bring herself to believe that he had left her for another. Powerless to learn anything about his fate, secretly she feared a more tragic explanation. Kirghyl Karakassian had often spoken of flying to arms against Frondism, someplace where the battle was not already lost in advance, as it was here. Perhaps he had gotten his chance to cross the boundary separating act from intention. And perhaps he lay at rest there, in the trenches, under the bombed-out debris, under the dust.

When they lay soft and warm, stretched out beside each other, or when they opened their eyes before dawn, sliding intertwined from dreams into darkness, he told her about the country where he had spent his childhood, a moor broken by mountains and peaked cliffs. Within those stark rocks, secret underground colonies had been established. The basalt was riddled with tunnels. Some of the passageways opened onto the south slope. The caverns there overlooked a stunning group of volcanoes. An intense blue shimmered inside their craters. In those moments when the viola player, with her clear timbre edged with sorrow, seemed as if she were dreaming, as if she saw nothing, instead she saw again, clearly, Kirghyl Karakassian. Again she felt the indescribable softness of his feathers; again she felt him against her body, her lips, her loins. A strange weakness brushed the crooks of her palms. Pressed against Kirghyl, she struggled against vertigo, she tried to lean out over the space where the void began. With him she contemplated the blue curls of blue lava; past the dark stumps of chimneys, she admired the burning turquoise lakes. After the music came an infinite silence. With Kirghyl Karakassian she followed the blue birds that soared soundlessly above blue prairies and blue mists.

A long way from Tchaki Estherkhan's breathtaking solos, this is also the story of Bieno Amirbekian, one of the best horse thieves of this century. Bieno, the brother of Matko Amirbekian, is twenty-nine years old. The lore of thievery was handed down to him from excellent teachers, some of whom had mustaches so luxurious that their ends could be pulled back and knotted under the nape. The cultivation and maintenance of such a magnificent mustache is not simply some folkloric fad. Rather, it is proof of a hard and laborious existence, free of error; proof that the mustache wearer has not been forced to undergo the owners' harsh punishments, the inconveniences of the judicial system, jail, the clippers. To the community of the initiated, such a mustache is a demonstration of pride and prowess.

Unlike his brother Matko, that mediocre thief already caught and shaven, Bieno has never spent any time in prison. He enjoys catching his mustache points in the corners of his mouth, as if he were champing a bit. His physique, like that of a shepherd from the steppes, radiates insolence and good cheer. Peasant women and farmers' wives go crazy for him, a fact that is not inconsequential for his professional success. All the members of the Amirbekian tribe, Bieno's uncles, cousins, sisters, grandmothers, ancestors—with the sole exception of Matko—have been remarkably adept in cultivating long mustaches. Bieno Amirbekian follows in their footsteps, even though some might reproach him for his frivolity, his lack of character, his naïve, rustic attraction to the big city.

Bieno Amirbekian has come to parade his manly silhouette around the capital. He has come to Chamrouche to spend thousands of coins, a fortune he made off the sale of some superb fillies, a herd that galloped obediently along narrow goat paths, across riverbeds and fields of scree, from one valley to the next, eight times in a single night. Now, drinking from morning to night, importuned by a court of tipsy partygoers and prostitutes, Bieno has wasted all his money in a few weeks. One day, he happens to notice the ominous building where his little brother Matko is locked up. Suddenly he remembers his duty as elder brother. He's been forgetting the principles of mutual aid and generosity that the Amirbekians have honored for generations. Remorse grabs him by the throat. Turning frugal, he snoops here and there as he strolls around Chamrouche with the intention of organizing Matko's escape. But no ideas come to him, and now he is penniless, an unsophisticated country boy in the fashionable neighborhoods as well as the rough ones. He doesn't like the underworld here, so different from the wholesome tribes of thieves. A gang leader laughs at him, a girl turns her back. He wanders from one arrondissement to the next, his mustache combed like a city dweller's, dressed like a lingerie salesman with a silk scarf knotted around his neck to hide the white scratch of a bullet scar, from a night back in the '80s when he got cornered by a militia of grooms.

On the sidewalk, the heat was intensifying. The three, Matko Amirbekian, Will MacGrodno, and Aram Bouderbichvili—the inept stallion-napper, the unrepentent bird, and the clumsy wrestler—the three ex-prisoners had divided up their fifteen cents, but they had not separated. They remained seated, facing the door of the sawmill. As the end of the lunch break approached, the workers came outside the workshop to smoke. The air was perfumed with tar and pine resin, the scent of new boards. Matko got up, crossed the street, and struck up a conversation with some men in overalls.

I remember Matko Amirbekian like it was yesterday. Twenty-three years old, but with the look of a teenager, mocking and a bit sad; black hair, curly despite the weekly scissor cuts; skin the color of overbaked bread, a bit floury from the years in prison; eyes a very bright lichen green, the iris darkening slightly toward the circumference, as if, somewhere inside his gaze, some big-sister sorceress had drawn a circle of kohl; a symmetrical face and, above the full lips, the beginnings of a mustache, the stubble of a deplorable thief just out of his apprenticeship and already caught with his hand in the bag, beaten, arrested, humiliated. I suppose he must have won women's hearts more successfully than he won over skittish horses; he must have stolen their kisses more easily than he managed to soothe wild tarpans, to mollify the wayward mares who whinnied and stamped, alerting sleepy guards, biting, waking the villagers, balking and pawing at the ground.

That twenty-seventh of May, a brilliant sun illuminated the heights of the capital.

Matko returned to his companions and held out a cigarette for each. One cigarette for the ex-prisoner Aram Bouderbichvili, one cigarette for the ex-prisoner Will MacGrodno. Matko himself was smoking one. He took shelter behind the cloud he exhaled from his lungs. His lashes meshed together to weave a second curtain, a protective screen between himself and the simple, too-luminous landscape of the street. After years in a cell, a man has trouble getting used to the brilliance of springtime, getting used to free space. All three men were still feeling the shock of their unexpected liberation. On this bit of sidewalk, perhaps even more than before, they felt dazed, incapable of euphoria or even a sincere good mood. Aram and Will MacGrodno, too, masked their confusion behind mute gray puffs. Will MacGrodno cleared his throat and spat. Beyond the entry, the woodworkers had gotten their circular saw going again and were bracing themselves against a cart full of yellow boards. Minute by minute, the industrial quarter was coming back to life. As the three men stubbed out their cigarettes, they could see that everything was in its place and functioning in Chamrouche, while they, with their asses parked on the stone ledge above the gutter, were sitting still, relegated outside the boundaries of normal life, with few ideas regarding their near future.

How could they start over? Breaking the silence, Will MacGrodno suggested that they set out in search of the Vanzetti Circus, where Aram had worked until the famous and ill-fated entanglement that had temporarily ended his career. The circus must be jolting around somewhere in the region, or in the countryside. They could find out the stops on the tour, catch up to it, and get themselves hired. Aram Bouderbichvili as wrestler, Matko Amirbekian as stableboy, maybe, and he, Will MacGrodno, as an acrobat or a clown. No echo seconded this proposition. Then Matko wondered out loud whether Will MacGrodno could renew contact with his network or his group, migrants who might help them reach foreign lands. Over there, in the ranks of those in the South, they could fight without hiding their faces. They could go into battle against Frondism, and with more than just their bare hands. Then Aram interrupted. He advised that, instead, Matko should look for his brother. At this very moment, no doubt, that expert on vanishing herds owned a farm or a livestock operation with flourishing stables. He would take all three of them on as employees.

A disconnected conversation made up of fantasies, built on nothing realistic. Aram had no desire to exhaust himself in the circus arena again, to risk his power, his athletic devotion, in the awkward grappling of giants from the crowd. Will MacGrodno, for his part, no longer possessed the keys to gain access to clandestine networks. As for Matko, after giving much serious thought while in the Central prison to the question of his vocation, he had lost his pastoral spirit. He showed little enthusiasm when he heard anything about horses, wild or otherwise, or about cattle that needed tending, in the backcountry boredom of the steppe.

Then Matko repeated the woodworkers' warning. Be careful, the rot is gathering strength again. The men in overalls had sketched out a picture of the political situation in Chamrouche that had been developing over the past few weeks. The war was too bogged down and distant, no longer victorious enough nor bloody enough to mobilize the masses. So instead of just watching nervously as their popularity decreased, the Frondists had adopted a new tactic: they were leaving the stage of government. The bigoted tirades stigmatizing the ragged enemies in the poor countries were abruptly suspended. The time had come to relight the torch of hatred at home. Internal enemies, no less ragged, had multiplied underground in the stronghold of Chamrouche. It was time for a radical cleansing here at home.

Now, one after another, the Frondists were abandoning the administrative posts where they had previously installed themselves. Upon their resignations, they signed decrees intended to poison their successors: amnesty for a thousand common law prisoners, for example, based on purely random criteria. In fact, it was obvious that they had placed their underlings in all the crucial positions of the State machine. Since April, they had begun to reinvigorate their furor by hitting the streets, just as they did during the good old days of their ascent. Officially they handed power over to the Parliamentarians, the elected National Democrats, the Social Nationalist Military. What party was that again? grumbled Aram Bouderbichvili. Same as ever, you can bet, Will MacGrodo sneered. The same, yes, under a different symbol, Matko confirmed. He continued his summary. While elected officials puffed up and strutted around, the Frondists controlled the show from behind the scenes, and in the street, they channeled the simmering crowds to their own ends.

There are days, Matko said, when they put on terrible festivals. Days when they declare open season on the vermin. They launch expeditions against birds, against intellectuals, against bums and drifters who take too long to present themselves at party headquarters for a card.

Hearing this, Will MacGrodno rose to his feet: They can keep waiting in their headquarters! I'm not going over there to get my talons stuck in a trap!

The story gets complicated here, because a writer gets mixed up in it, and when he can find nothing good about the world from any perspective, the writer, Iakoub Khadjbakiro, takes his paper and transforms the fabric of truth. He is not content to offer peevish, bitter pronouncements about the world that surrounds him. He does not reproduce in exact detail the elemental brutality to which humanity has been reduced, the bestial tragedy of their fate. Such a procedure would swiftly leave him disgusted; he would grow weary of it. He would compose only little anecdotal scenarios, mediocre embellishments of a mediocre reality. He would take no pleasure in his art, and soon he would stop writing altogether. Instead, he selects only the most tenuous, shadowy, and harmonious threads from real life, and he interweaves them with his memory, with the cherished visions that come to him as he sleeps; he weaves them with his past, with the impatience and errors and betrayed beliefs of his childhood. In his head he takes what he has seen and reshapes it, reconstitutes it according to his whim.

In his books, Iakoub Khadjbakiro's usual process was to replace the hideousness of current events with his own absurd images. His own partial hallucinations, both troubled and troubling. Most of the time, although obviously not always, he obeyed the rules of logic. He depicted the contemporary world, he reflected his personal experience in his words, he examined his generation, how they had sabotaged themselves by giving up and letting go. He believed that dreams contained indispensable keys to understanding the state of the world, appreciating the historical basis for current events and the moral level where humanity had been stagnating for centuries.

This is why he included vast oneiric parts of the universe in his analysis of things. Onto his portraits of men and women he grafted somnambulatory behaviors, nocturnal modes of thought. He gave his characters whimsical, nearly mad schemes. Iakoub Khadjbakiro seemed to work in abstract phantasmagoria, but suddenly his exotic parallel worlds would coincide with something buried in some random person's unconscious mind. Suddenly, that reader would emerge from the subterranean levels of mirage and onto the main square of the capital. In the middle of Chamrouche, with its busy, banal everyday life, and along with the thousand-year-old cancers still active in everyone, that reader would see ancient barbarisms, ancient regressions. Exotic is the term applied to aberrant, yet fundamental, particles of matter.

Reading one of Iakoub Khadjbakiro's novels often means traveling with no safety equipment, in grave danger, across the hauntings and shames of our time, into the heart of what other people repress and deny. Into the heart of Chamrouche's bad dreams. But Iakoub Khadjbakiro was also living out his own story. It could be outlined as follows: he suffered from composing works that conformed little to the public taste, texts for lost birds, filled with enigmas that few of his readers unraveled, works with no guarantee of success that attracted the disapproval of Frondist authorities. He would have liked to construct a more effective book, one where poetry was no barrier between him and his denunciation of the dominant ideology, a work without gaps, without chimeras, without disjunction. He was planning to dedicate all his powers to it, to sacrifice the relative peace of his existence. But he was unable to render on paper, without metaphors, his disgust, the nausea that seized him when he faced the present day and the inhabitants of that present. Besides, for him, writing according to the style of the day, according to the rules in force, corresponded to a laziness that he did not want sullying his conscience. It corresponded to capitulation before the form, the colors, the breath, the intelligence, the sensibilities, and the mendacious language of a system in which nothing was innocent or unpolluted.

With Iakoub Khadjbakiro, we approach the story of a man who lives in the anguish of being unclear, a man who spends twenty-four hours a day obsessed by the real, but who nevertheless expresses himself in an esoteric, sibylline manner, locating his heroes in nebulous societies and unrecognizable times.

Of his most readable book, yet to come, he had not yet sketched out anything but the final scene.

Iakoub Khadjbakiro had loved a few women over the course of his life, and in particular Dojna Magidjamalian, Hakatia Badrinourbat, and Vassila Temirbekian. As in the theater, Dojna, then Hakatia, then Vassila, one after another, walked from separate entrances onto the desolate set of this final scene, which he had long imagined in the midst of nature, on the edge of a forest or in a clearing, but which he was bringing closer and closer to himself, setting it in Chamrouche, somewhere in the center of the capital. The behavior of these three women was strange and he could make no sense of it from a novelistic perspective. Iakoub Khadjbakiro wanted them to return to the far corners of the scene, and he planned, with a certain solemnity, to pay close attention to their faces, each one different yet somber and very beautiful, the faces of three women past their youth, transfigured by the ordeals that Frondism had forced them to undergo. Without fear, he would linger over those features, which would become symbols of the world, at once full of hope and washed of all hope. Then Dojna would lift her head and begin, softly, to sing a slow, spacious song of boundless sadness, and Hakatia, after remaining silent, would sing with her in tertian harmony, and soon Vassila would join them. The melody would have no spectacular character if not this: building as if it would never stop, within the center of a silent and fixed space. This is how Iakoub Khadjbakiro wanted to close the novel that he was failing to write: on a fermata. On a fermata that no one would ever want to break.

This is also the story of two Frondists, who seem identical in every way. Actually, three, five hundred, a thousand. They are legion, millions. Many more than two. Their number can be explained by economic and social factors, but it takes courage to complete the explanation, to say that something instinctive, doubtless inscribed in the genetic heritage of the species, compels the great masses of humanity to condone that which promises desolation and carnage. A mysterious collective impulse activates minds and steers them toward the worst. All it takes is the designation of an enemy outside the border, and in a single night, public opinion will turn to screaming for war and solidarity with our soldiers; a single day of orchestrating the lie is enough for public opinion to endorse bomb strikes and demand victory at any price, to swallow martial propaganda in greedy gulps. When tribunals identify scapegoats within the borders, the crowds stand with stitched lips before crimes, or even become radicalized, falling madly in love with the loudest voices, longing for a new springtime of genocide. The Frondists' success is also built on their leaders' prominence. After a period of pure and simple savagery, these leaders work out thousand-year plans. They choose subtle tactics, integrating ideas for the long term and even for permanence. Among the most striking figures of this new generation, one man stands out: Balynt Zagoebel, whose cunning, violence, and lack of scruples inflame the party's followers.

The attacks that decimate his family attract compassion from a large number of supporters and help to harden his determination. Balynt Zagoebel's father, an industrialist in chemicals and armaments, is killed in a bomb attack by two unknown persons. Although traveling in an armored car, Balynt Zagoebel's wife and son fall in an ambush, pecked to death by birds. Beginning in the late '6os, Zagoebel can be considered the most solid, the most shrewd, the least susceptible to pity, of all the cogs in the totalitarian machinery. It was his idea to withdraw from power. Nothing threatens the Party, all the levers of the State are at his command, but he placed the legal institutions back in the hands of patriot-clowns and social-puppets. For himself, he kept the street, the press, the police, the lively sympathies of the general staff, of the active-duty sub-officers, of industry. Now no cracks can weaken the steel of Frondism. If there are setbacks in the war against the South, or some bad outcomes in commerce or agriculture, these cannot be blamed on him. Smug puppets now legislate and administrate in the government. Of these characters, people will remember the three-piece suits, the well-polished shoes; people will admire the extensive vocabulary, the patrician authority, although a little diminished by senile wavering, one must admit. School directors rush to sing their praises. Their speeches before the Chamber are retransmitted on the airwaves, and perhaps the microphones are to blame for a slight tendency toward a pathetic tremolo. Some of them comb gray toupees over their skulls, in an effort to appeal to the eighteen- to thirty-two-year-old demographic.

But we were speaking of Zagoebel. Balynt Zagoebel is a man of the '40s, and so he will remain until he dies. Until then, he will continue to wear old-fashioned clothes, long trench coats, kidskin gloves. He will never cease to style himself as a man of the shadows. He will persist in his habits, raising them to the level of legend. He will scribble orders and speeches in the same eternal spiral notebook. He will plunge his hands into beige leather coat pockets; regardless of the weather he will give the impression of being dressed for autumn, for travel, for night. His smile will be reserved for his own jokes, which he will sometimes prepare in advance, and sometimes not, but they will never fail to include some odious element calculated to rouse the masses. As the years go by, he will perpetuate a Frondist tone, a

Frondist manner, a Frondist attitude, which will be no more than a veneer of the '40s over the end of the century, over the planet. Balynt Zagoebel's physiognomy will appeal to millions of people until his death. It will awaken memories in them, simultaneously calling up images of their teacher, their auto repair man, their foreman, recalling a film actor, a '50s movie star whose name and films they have forgotten: an ordinary, familiar head, then, and at the same time a head associated with the magic of darkened theaters.

With an unmatched understanding of glory, Balynt Zagoebel does not show himself in public too often. Only on those occasions when he suspects that history will remember the date. When the winds turn bitter, and it becomes expedient to rail against troublemakers and decadence. Most of the time, someone else takes his place and riles up the crowd. A faithful old friend, who seems to come from the same '40s rear commission, who has the same voice as his, the same tics, the same supply of jokes to stoke the cruel hilarity of the masses surrounding him, the same aging movie-star rictus, the same spiral notebook, the same name. Yes, a perfect double: Balynt Zagoebel.

The three ex-prisoners had been shifting course from one street to the next and had finally gotten away from the prison and the industrial zone. Since they hadn't paid much attention to direction in their rambling, they had gotten lost. They were walking slowly through a peaceful arrondissement. Without knowing it, they passed under the windows of the writer Iakoub Khadjbakiro.

Farther on, they began looking for the way to a young workers' hostel where Will MacGrodno thought they could get a room for the night. They had planned, had discussed, on a street corner. They did not dare say a word to any of the inhabitants. They were stuck on that street corner and, a few meters away, some little girls were playing hopscotch. On the sun-soaked sidewalk the girls had traced the squares with a piece of chalk, likely stolen from a classroom, and now they were hopping on one foot, bickering, not laughing. Above them hung a Party flag. The house behind the bouncing little girls was a Frondist place, perhaps a meetinghouse, or a hygiene patrol office. Aram, Matko, and Will MacGrodno had turned swiftly in the opposite direction.

Next they had ended up in Chamrouche's central business district, passing luxury boutiques and fashionable cinemas, one after another. The boulevards were teeming. Intimidated, the three of them emitted not a single sound. They dedicated their energy to offending no one, avoiding the pedestrians who plowed past them, who assessed them as a negligible quantity. Many of these walkers wore the deadened sneers of the well fed, the kind of physically fit bodies acquired in clubs for gymnastics or tae kwon do. They came and went, some looking unhappy, others, on the contrary, shining with triumphant contempt. It was easy to imagine them watching one of Balynt Zagoebel's rallies, suddenly touched by the grace of camaraderie and spewing their own rancor into the general roar, raising their arms in furious slant salutes along with thousands just like them, finally overcome with love, these richly perfumed people, for their neighbors' fried-potato stench, intoxicated in the heart of the multitude, ready to depart instantly to wherever they were sent, ready to offer up their blood and if necessary to wade in the blood of others, to die and to kill, to flush out the vermin of this world.

That was why, in those years of the late '80s, the atmosphere held hints of the '50s or even the '40s, with gleams of leather jackets and a thick, slightly bestial quality, like the pungent wake of hunting dogs and their masters.

Will MacGrodno feels irritated, uncomfortable. All three of them are hungry. They decide to grab a bite in a café. They head down a less turbulent cross street. There's a modern-looking establishment, decorated with a plastic material that imitates and is hard to tell from marble. From inside, the windows look like they've been washed with a plaster-soaked rag. Streaks glisten like voluminous entangled serpents in the sunlight. There's only one customer, a well-dressed young man next to the entry, slowly sipping a cup of tea with lemon. The three men lean against the counter, where prices are cheaper. As they wait for a server, they play a game. They make a pile of the temporary identification papers they got from the court secretary at the prison. They mix them up, and each man takes an ID at random. To Will MacGrodno fall the papers of Aram Bouderbichvili; as for Aram, he's become a bird; and Matko remains Matko Amirbekian.

It's not an employee who comes through the service door but the owner, a squat, chubby-cheeked man with greasy hair and glasses. He has barely looked at his three new customers when his face blotches with hostile color.

Don't you know how to read? he asks. And his sausage-like finger with its blackened nail points toward the sign hanging above the percolator: NO NEGS AND NO SPADGERS WILL BE SERVED IN THIS ESTABLISHMENT.

We'd like three ham sandwiches, says Matko.

That's what I thought. So you can't read, says the owner. You can try your luck somewhere else. We don't serve negs here.

Aram shrugs. In spite of prison, he has maintained his wrestler's physique. He dedicated half the time in his cell to pull-ups, sit-ups, and other exercises to build muscle and flexibility. Even when the small space hampered every effort, even when the toilet stench robbed him of any desire to respect his own body. That stubborn activity prevented him from slouching or getting bitter. He flexes his pectorals, spreads his arms, and places them on the bar, and without aggression, he says: My name is Will MacGrodno and I am not a neg. We would like three ham sandwiches and a pitcher of water.

Will MacGrodno, in his turn, leans against the chrome-plated handrail protecting the fake plastic marble. Will MacGrodno does not have Aram's professional calm. His voice trembles with indignation as he snaps: My name is Aram Bouderbichvili. I suppose that name might mean something to you?

The owner retreats against his bottles, but he doesn't look impressed. Years have gone by since the business at the Vanzetti Circus. He probably doesn't remember anything about it. He whistles between his teeth with meditative malice and shakes his head. Ignoring Will MacGrodno, he measures the wrestler's herculean silhouette from the corner of his eye. He can only see the upper half, the impassive face, the green-checked shirt, which is enough, by itself, to proclaim Aram's origin in the inexhaustible class of poor suckers.

Listen here. What did you say your name was? Will MacGrodzing? Is that it?

MacGrodno, Aram corrects.

That's a neg name, the owner declares. Your name is Bill Mac-Grodzing, you say? Then you're a neg. And your friends are, too. Now get the fuck out of here, or I'm calling the police.

All three of them stare at him. Each in his way. Matko Amirbeki-an directs the emerald splendor of his free man's gaze, he blinks his eyes, just once, and encloses the owner in a magic circle of kohl. Will MacGrodno stares daggers from under his furrowed eyebrows, stabbing the owner thoroughly from the hairline to the folds of his double chin. Aram Bouderbichvili's eyes have narrowed slightly, as they always do just before a fist gets thrown. Matko is first to pivot toward the exit. The others follow. They have no desire to discuss the incident, and they no longer have any desire to sit on the sidewalk, either.

The noise of the capital envelops them: the rhythm of footsteps, echoes of conversations, buses shifting gears, trucks, advertisements, squealing brakes. Matko remains Matko, but now Aram isn't quite sure if he's Aram Bouderbichvili again or if he's still Will MacGrodno. Will MacGrodno makes no effort to hide how shaken he is. His mouth has a sinister twist as he spits. A solitary phrase scampers around inside his skull. It hops, jabbers, bangs against all the exits but does not manage to burst out: I suppose that name means something to you? Doesn't that name mean anything to you?

They go on, another fifty meters. They're joined by the man who, a few moments ago, was sipping tea as he studied the coiled, plastery boa constrictors inscribed like a watermark on the café window. He has the bronze complexion of a southerner, but now he looks pale. He catches up to them and stops. All of them stop.

You know, not everyone's as bad as that guy, he says. I'm a neg, too, in a way. I wouldn't want you to believe everyone thinks like them.

His fine lips quiver, struck with emotion. The three men notice that he stutters over the word *neg*, a term that only a true, dyed-in-the-wool Frondist could pronounce without qualm. His hesitant yet sincere solidarity is a balm for the heart. His name is Dimirtchi Makionian, and he's a cellist. He asks if they need money, and, even though this question is offered without condescension, in the most fraternal manner possible, they answer proudly that everything is fine in that area. So the cellist gives them a gift. He offers each of them a ticket to the concert set for that very night, the twenty-seventh of May, at eight o'clock. Unfortunately, he is not certain that the concert will take place.

Have you seen the posters? he asks, worried.

All four of them together go looking for a poster announcing the evening's concert. In downtown Chamrouche, there are notice boards covered with advertisements for cultural events, shows, programs, subscriptions. The four plunge back into the chaotic currents, through avenues bordered with houses where millionaires live. They find the poster. They find two of them. The first lists the members of the quartet, the Djylas Quartet. Ansaf Vildan, violin. Mourtaza Tchopalav, violin. Tchaki Estherkhan, viola. Tchaki? Matko interrupts, for this is both a girl's name and a boy's name. A woman, Dimirtchi clarifies, an amazing musician. The best viola player in Chamrouche. Dimirtchi Makionian, cello. Insulting graffiti mars the second poster. The name of Kaanto Djylas has been crossed out. ROAST THE SPADGERS, someone has written. And obscenities, a gang symbol, the phone number for an answering service.

The three are happy to have Dimirtchi Makionian at their side. This morning, when they opened their eyes in the prison's filthy dawn, their future looked like a drudgery of cleaning hallways, and now here they are, standing on the grand boulevards, chatting amiably with a famous musician.

The fate of the concert interests them.

It's not really our group that they're angry at right now, explains

Dimirtchi Makionian. Their hostility is all directed at the composers on the program. Djylas, Ichkouat, Naïsso Baldakchan. Do you know them?

Do you like them?

Will MacGrodno confesses their triple ignorance. Then he dares to whisper the truth, to justify their lack of culture, to reveal exactly where they've come from. Why they feel so foreign, today, on the street. The cellist smiles with an almost guilty expression. His gaze passes over each of them, welcoming one after the other.

You'll like it, he promises. Baldakchan. He's best known for his works for female voices. His poem for vocal trio and orchestra. It's amazing. He was a genius, but he was stifled here, he had to expatriate. Then he came back to Chamrouche. Exile was hard on him. He came back to commit suicide. You'll see, his quartet never leaves anyone cold. I bet my right hand, you'll love it.

Around them, men walk stiffly, their chins tucked, accompanied by pretty women cinched into '50s trench coats.

Let's not draw a crowd, the cellist advises, and he guides them off to one side. Naïsso Baldakchan, he says. Kaanto Djylas, Tamian Ichkouat. They're negs. All negs. And my friends are, too.

At four o'clock in the afternoon, at the same time that Dimirtchi Makionian and the three ex-prisoners were getting acquainted, two trucks and a dark blue car entered the potholed street leading to the Vanzetti Circus, in which the clown Baxir Kodek was one of the attractions. A circus, after several seasons on tour in the provinces, always tries to close its journey with at least one season in the area around the capital. The audience is the same as in towns hundreds and even thousands of kilometers distant from Chamrouche, but the carnies are unanimous in their desire for that cyclical reappearance in a place that adds, so they believe, a certain prestige to their work. Vanzetti had decided to reinstall his company in the suburbs of Chamrouche. For the year to come, the caravan would limit its movements to the densely populated areas around the great capital crown.

The trucks and car jolted carefully up to the big top, circled around it, passed the menagerie and its cages, and came to a halt before the trailers. The grass across the uneven terrain was bleaching under the dust and sun. The animals were asleep in their cages. Far away, the city hummed, a continuous murmur punctuated with sirens that wailed very distinctly despite the distance, sirens of police cars and fire trucks. Here, in this less densely constructed zone, calm reigned. The artists were out of sight. No doubt some of them were practicing their numbers under the unlit tent, in the rings that stank of death, cold sweat, and meat for beasts. Others must have left for an excursion into Chamrouche, or else they were dozing inside their wheeled homes.

I have always been struck by the atmosphere of grimy disarray that creeps through carnival grounds during the daytime hours. Not even the slightest magic on that wrong side of the set, only tarps, ropes, wooden posts with a thousand dents. Even if the ticket booth has just been freshly painted, even if, in honor of the capital and its citizens, the illusionists and animal trainers have washed all the equipment from top to bottom, only a horribly stale version of the evening magic appears. Old leotards and trunks in faded colors hang above the sinks; outside the stable, the ladder for climbing up to the trick rider's quarters is stuck sideways in the mud; deep in their lightless corners, sealed in with plywood and shit, bored beasts ruminate and rumble. Every detail attests to a sad contradiction of the lie. The absence of mystery becomes overwhelming, there is nothing more to sustain the melancholy, the memories from childhood. With a sudden brush against this miserable version of reality, abruptly forced to touch the rotting corpse, you're a grown-up, and you let the shame lay you out.

This atmosphere did not move the visitors.

The truck drivers dropped down onto the grass. After twice activating a siren, the car's driver got out, soon imitated by his passenger, a big man whose dark, shiny hair was slightly mussed from riding with open windows down the beltway, just a few strands blown astray, like egret plumes. The man looked like an egret, like a raptor; but raptors of this kind are not birds. His beige leather coat, with its exceptional quality and luxurious texture, betrayed his belonging to a very different race. The driver, too, wore expensive, even elegant clothes, although intentionally old-fashioned. The two motorists headed toward a yellow trailer. This one was as good as any other; they had selected it at random.

Since the truck drivers knew they weren't immediately needed, they decided to go test the lions' apathy.

Baxir Kodek was finishing his afternoon nap when Sarvara Dradjia, the dwarf, knocked on his door and entered. She was escorted by two characters who looked like skinny giants standing behind her.

The clown had heard the car's siren, but he had not rushed to the window to see what was happening. In his half-slumber, he had thought: Death. That's death sounding its horn. And now Sarvara Dradjia was catching her breath and trembling near the table, and now, from his bunk, he perceived the hard features of the men she had guided to him, and he said to himself: Just after blowing its trumpet, death found the den where I was hiding from it. Sarvara mouthed a mute prayer in his direction. He got up to meet the intruders, paused to draw the dwarf close against him. His serenity was contagious. Under his hand, she relaxed a little. The envoys of death remained stationed on the last step. In the menagerie, the lions were growling irritably.

Vanzetti isn't here, I'm told?

No, the clown confirmed. He's in town.

The false raptor had his hands in his pockets. He pulled them out. Now he was holding a spiral notebook and a considerable wad of cash. He spoke.

The little woman told me you'd act as interim director. But it doesn't matter. The main thing is that we're talking to someone who can help us out. Long story short, here's what brings us. You had a show planned for tonight? Good. We'll buy all the seats. At full price. A great deal for Vanzetti. So he won't go around complaining afterward that we didn't treat him fairly.

The upright egret reeled off his words with the imperious tone of a landlord threatening to evict a bad tenant. His little spiral notebook was open and he referred to it with quick glances, as if the phrases he shot out could have been suggested by abbreviations or numbers that he had assembled on some previous day, in anticipation of this very moment.

I'll add a nice bonus to that, he said. Never forget to tip your entertainment, that's our policy.

The wad of money landed on the wrinkled plaid blanket covering the clown's bed. The bills composed a compact, purple volume. They looked new.

I'm truly sorry, Baxir Kodek began.

The man cut him off.

Fine. In exchange—because after all, we are going to ask the artists for something in exchange—you will perform an outdoor show for us, wherever we tell you. Okay? That's all clear, then. You represent popular culture. And we support popular culture.

Baxir Kodek caressed Sarvara Dradjia's shoulder, where her arm began. A silent communication formed between them. The dwarf transmitted her anxiety, her sharp presentiment of disaster; the clown tried to convince her not to succumb to her terror. Under light fabric, Baxir could feel the strap of Sarvara Dradjia's bra, the almost childlike softness of her flesh. With his hand he told her that these people did not exist, that they were, at most, animated trench coats, manufactured beings who had been delegated by millions of very ordinary men and women to radiate, in public, in the name of all, death. In order to calm Sarvara, he managed once again to feign courage. Inside him rose the cries of a baying beast; he could see criminal intent glowing like a halo around this smooth-talking egret's brain; he felt a desire to convulse without restraint, to kneel like vanquished prey, but, with a squeeze of his hand, he explained to Sarvara that they must not give in to fear.

I am sorry, he refused. I cannot make this decision for Vanzetti. In any case, from a technical standpoint, what you're proposing is impossible. I apologize, gentlemen. Perhaps you could leave your contact information? An address? A telephone number? Vanzetti . . .

There was a moment of confusion. A floating stupefaction. Then the raptor peeled his lips off his gums, displaying an ironic pout, and whistled. But what's the deal with this circus? What's up with this sparrow here?

His companion let out a nasty huff. He contemplated Baxir with a professional killer's rigid obedience, as if he might pull a pistol out of his coat at any moment and shoot anything alive inside the trailer. With a flick of his fingers, the raptor subdued his stray egret's plumage. Instantly he took on the appearance of an actor from a '50s movie, a neorealist star from the years when black and white still competed with color.

If Vanzetti objects, you'll send him to us, okay? admonished the envoy of death, the envoy of a million very ordinary men and women, the raptor, the actor, the neorealist star, the Frondist leader, Balynt Zagoebel.

Okay, good. Now, get a move on. In forty-five minutes, everything you have will be loaded into trucks, all the acrobats and equipment that can be moved. We'll leave the animals behind. Technical reasons, as you said. I want jugglers, clowns, tightrope walkers, fire eaters, your freaks, and your band. Popular culture, get it? We don't care about Vanzetti, we're putting you in charge. You recognize me, right? So there's no problem. We're leaving here in forty-five minutes. You'll have time to get everything set up over there. For a great show. We're putting our faith in you to provide the ambiance, the pizzazz, the party. The money is there, everything is in order. We always support popular culture. See? Always and forever.

Behind Balynt Zagoebel's back, there was the uneven terrain, Vanzetti's white wagon, the killer, the echo of angry lions, of horses pawing at their straw.

Baxir made a powerless gesture, bent down, sat, and rested his hands on Sarvara Dradjia's hips. Next to him he could feel her unbearable fear. Sarvara's gaze was riveted desperately to Baxir's. Since the wrestler, Aram Bouderbichvili, had gotten packed off to prison, the dwarf had become the clown's confidante. She alone knew that Baxir had no taste for the circus, that the sorrowful cruelty of his work constantly devoured him. She alone knew his personal definition of Frondism. Frondism, he had confided, is when you're beaten in front of a crowd and you fall, and the crowd laughs until they cry. Frondism wasn't something that a few evil leaders invented; it was a natural expression of the crowd. It was evident that Frondism was yet another thing, as well. Baxir had crouched down to Sarvara's height and consoled her with a big smile, as one consoles a very small girl rather than a woman, bringing his face and his gaze close to hers, holding within them all the hope and all the faith in the world.

Frondism is also a lark mirror. Across the most varied social spectrum, its flashes attract and hypnotize, its facets distort and entrap. Between one flicker and the next, the larks become exhilarated, their judgment suspended. Fluttering they drop, lightly they rebound, incapable of modifying, refusing, or changing the trajectory they've been assigned. As they sing they give themselves up, by the hundreds, the thousands, the millions. But larks are not birds. For proof take Bieno Amirbekian, the legendary horse thief. Bieno has been recruited by the Frondists.

Here is a man raised to uprightness by the entire Amirbekian clan: rebellious uncles, intractable aunts and cousins who never, from puberty to the grave, accepted even the slightest brush of a razor. Here is a boy educated by fathers who taught him the ropes of his vocation and inscribed, deep inside his skull, a love for lands without borders, a hatred of barriers, of barbed wire or any other kind; here is a babe rocked by mothers who lulled him to sleep with hymns to freedom, jeering at the rich owners, the powerful figures of city and countryside. From his first days he knew that irreparable shame would fall upon the clan if one of its members went over to the wrong side, in armed service to the owners.

Bieno's story has already been outlined. In the dive bars of Chamrouche, Bieno Amirbekian wasted all his moral standing, along with his savings. He thought he was having fun when the prostitutes admired the curve of his neck as he laughed, when they adored his eyes that sparkled emerald and quartz, sighed over his incomparable mustache, his slightly gritty horseman's voice. But this time came swiftly to an end. Without coins jingling in his pockets, friendships in the city's underworld dissolved in two days. Bieno was bereft. Solitude and penury made him less and less stable.

At the end of April, a drunk invites him to a neighborhood meeting. Bieno goes without hesitation, with the idea that mixing with the Frondists might help clarify his plans for the future. He thinks about helping his little brother Matko escape, but what strikes the observer most about Bieno is that his head is empty.

So here is Bieno Amirbekian entering a committee office; he catches the enthusiasm in the room, applauds, and yells along with it, carried away with its trouble and grief, riding its virulence. Here is Bieno Amirbekian, adopted by a branch of the Party, friend of the police, soon enjoying the advantages that the Frondist solidarity network provides. His look of an epic knight on horseback plays in his favor. Higher-ups in trench coats take note. They offer him a job, in exchange for a few minor aesthetic concessions. All too pleased to see himself promoted into the ranks of the elite corps, Bieno shaves off his mustache without a second's hesitation. In exchange for a few rough cuts, he reports directly to none other than Balynt Zagoebel.

Here he is, Bieno Amirbekian, proud of his own image, the flash of his reflection, mirrored by his comrades in armbands. The sun is shining, everything is glittering. Bieno cackles near the truck, which has just disgorged a hygiene patrol into the neighborhood near the docks. A beautiful day, this twenty-seventh of May. A big popular rally is planned for the evening, and already Bieno is taking his position. For lack of horses, here he is capturing birds. Without them, this show for the masses risks a certain lack of excitement.

That one hanging around those crates over there, should we grab him? someone asks.

That one? All birdy feathers and neggy skin, under his fancy raincoat, his companion answers. And they all burst out laughing.

Bieno doubles over with laughter. Bieno Amirbekian, a good Frondist.

It's hot. Ragojine is enjoying the afternoon calm. He's delaying the moment when he must return to his ruined dwelling, to the rafters and their covering of powdery soot, the decor of clandestine disaster with the black windowpanes, the spiderwebs, the staircase where he sits at the top, shivering through the night. For the moment he prefers to relax outside, in the sunshine. He's wandering along next to the water. He has helped, just now, to load barrels of fuel oil onto a barge. He received a cent in exchange. Since the inclined ramp on which the barrels rolled had a very modest slope, he has not damaged his shoulder. The state of the wound is no worse. Strangely, it's even a bit less bad than it was this morning, when the fever had its hooks in him. Today he has eaten his fill. He imagines suddenly that life, at that moment, is worth the trouble of living. The atmosphere is springlike and no cold breeze forces him, but out of habit, he retightens the rope that belts his overly ample coat.

He notices a cigarette, bends in half to pick it up, and, when he stands up again, the sun blinds him. It's also the effect of a brief vertigo, caused by digesting raw fish. He leans back against a post and closes his eyes. He thinks of a strange country that he has already seen in dreams, a labyrinth of mountains with volcanoes bubbling among them. He has a sensation of being unconscious for an immeasurable time. He was assigned a grotto that opened in the sharply sloped bowl of a crater. Now awake, he watches the swirls of blue lava. Farther off, he can see valleys covered in fumaroles and blue heather. He breathes the evening's perfumes, the gusts of indigo sulphur, the clouds. Very close by, a stranger whispers a series of words that he does not understand, not even a syllable, in a language he has never heard before. A friend. She touches his cheek, his side, with an immense tenderness. Even if it isn't really your own kind who welcome you, he thinks, to be worthy of this gesture, this caress, dying is not such a high price.

When he opens his eyes again, he is not dead, but he is not surrounded by his own kind either. Well-built shadows circle and sway around him, hands in their pockets, like penguins. But penguins are not birds.

Again he closes his eyes.

I WENT TO PICK UP DOJNA MAGIDJAMALIAN at her apartment.
Dojna lived close to the theater, in the third arrondissement. She had
asked me to ring around seven o'clock; that way we would have time
to drink a cup of tea and talk about old times, when we were young.
We had agreed that, after the concert, we would go out for dinner
somewhere. As I reached the center of Chamrouche, I admit, I felt an
exaltation much like the headiness of my teen years. I had always
remained very much in love with Dojna, even during the nine years
that I lived with Vassila Temirbekian. Vassila's illness and then death
created a chasm between Dojna and me, an irrational, unjust chasm,
for we had no reason to feel guilty, but that chasm was ambiguous
enough that years passed before it was filled. Then, finally, we recon-
nected. Tribulation and maturity had modified the character of our
relationship. Dojna was more like a sister than a mistress: a passionately admired and respected sister. I left it to her to initiate the carnal
episodes of our relationship, those half-weeks and hot nights whose

limits and dates she alone chose in some unpredictable manner, and I hoarded them inside myself like treasures of happiness. I walked along with a joyful stride, my mind captivated by images of some sleepy embrace that might perhaps end our evening. Arriving on the square outside the theater, I ran across several men wearing trench coats, then I saw trucks parked in a side street. Just in front of the theater's grand staircase, some people were busily setting up a tarp and iron posts. Traffic was already interrupted at that time, twenty minutes to seven. The whole area was swarming with Frondists: without armbands, with armbands, in street clothes, in uniform, in trench coats, gray, khaki, wrinkled or neat as pins, innocent as children, haughty, nonchalant. They were getting ready for a demonstration, and my first reaction was to hope that it would move off by eight o'clock, that when the concert began, the procession would already be screaming its chants through other arteries of the capital. Then I suspected the Party might be planning a boycott of the concert: I remembered that the program included several composers liable to irritate the ideologues' delicate sensibilities. Kaanto Djylas, for example. Although he died before the time of the great brown victories, the old man had frequently expressed his opposition to the crusades against the poor countries that were just beginning, already taking shape in small-scale military operations. Through exile and suicide, Naïsso Baldakchan had twice broken with Chamrouche. As for Tamian Ichkouat, he had been the object of a smear campaign in the early '60s, when a handful of provinces were still resisting the tentacles of power. The intellectual dregs of Chamrouche spread false, racist smears about him—about him and his wife, whom they accused of being a swallow, since she was a foreigner, an enemy. The players' "neg" names were also, I think, something that stiffened up the Frondists' patriotic spines. A little colossus in a motorcycle jacket came up and, intentionally, bumped into me. I jumped away, assailed with the sort of physical anguish that I always experience when confronted with the raw aggression of people who want to hurt you but avoid looking you in the face. Although utterly bereft of subtlety, thugs have an instinctive ability to identify those who aren't on their side. Something strange about my walk or my manner must have alerted the little colossus, and he felt compelled to warn me that the street, on this evening, did not belong to decadents of my kind. The street, the square before the theater, had been annexed by a dull, colorless population that even the glow of the setting sun could not manage to paint more brightly. The trucks were blocking access to the square, transforming it into an arena bordered with buildings, an outdoor theater whose stage corresponded to the lawns and rows of box trees, whose seats corresponded to the steps where I stood petrified, gawking, attempting to understand the plot being woven. Groups were moving around in the buildings' upper-story windows, preparing to loose the banners of Frondism, inevitable wherever the masses concentrated in one place: burgundy red, mouse gray, and, in the center of a blinding white circle, the heavy black claws of their symbol, a slightly stylized, crook-legged spider, with which they identified fervently. The militants were unfurling these gigantic flags, anchored with the active collaboration of the buildings' occupants. Once the flags were hung, once this solemn decoration was brought to term, one could imagine what the atmosphere was like in those apartments, where it would be forbidden to light a lamp: like the entrails of a dirigible, in those old bourgeois salons with their balconies bagged, bathing in the winey twilight. Smaller panels and canvases already hung in various places throughout the square, but nothing adorned the theater's façade. Preparations like these left no trace of doubt: the Frondists were gathering here not to organize the starting point of a march but for a rally. So the concert was in danger of being significantly affected, euphemistically speaking. Even if the declared objective was not to sabotage our evening of chamber music, even if the orchestra connoisseurs, as the newspapers say, could get there without any trouble, the subtle notes of a string quartet could not easily compete with the great din outside: the howling thousands unleashed and amplified in the microphones, while the ringleaders snarled their hysteria to the crowd. Eight trucks were already topped with speakers, promising echoes just as mind-numbing as the speeches. Party technicians were reliable: there would be no breakdowns, no respite from all the electromagnetically transfigured spewings. A well-disciplined swarm, that was what the square looked like right now. Each technician had a task to complete and was completing it efficiently, without hurry, without flub. Planted in the middle of the grand staircase, which the militant teams had apparently neglected, a pack of curious onlookers stood staring. I was one of these anonymous fragments. Next to me, no eyes betrayed any disapproval; it is true that we had all learned to censor our emotions, in public and elsewhere. I continued to observe the operations. Brass trombones, trumpets, a tuba, sat shining on the sidewalk below. Frondists with sweat-stained armpits were almost done unloading the instruments from a vehicle parked nearby. Between a lamppost and the high window of a corner house some carnies were beginning to stretch a steel cable. The lamppost loomed over the corner of the staircase where I was standing. The cable ended fifteen meters farther off, at the second floor of the house. Its line looked problematic, not quite horizontal. The carnies worked on poorly balanced ladders, on truck roofs serving as platforms. They were clearly anxious and dissatisfied with this kind of improvisation. Twenty or so trench coats, and as many shirts with armbands, admonished the carnies to hurry up, considering their objections with more coldness than ill will. They were scolding, but they were helping. Other technicians, experts in electricity, connected spotlights to the power supply with cables. Inside a large moving van, I could make out clowns and acrobats getting dressed: sequined fabrics, multicolored jackets, stars. A couple of dwarves in blue overalls were clearing space on the street and sidewalk beneath the perilous, hanging path of the tightrope walkers. Bit by bit, the logical structure of the whole was revealed. A theatrical set would be marked out in front of the theater's grand staircase. Platforms and connecting walkways were arranged on the roofs of two or three vehicles, around a circular area whose axis on the ground coincided with the line the tightrope walkers would follow as they twirled. The small central square would disappear under the multitudes. The larger square would look like a crater, without exit, between rooftops flowing with decorations and banners. At strategic points on the buildings' façades, balconies would hold batteries of spotlights, loudspeakers, and, somewhere in the midst of this profusion, the platform where the orators would give their speeches, whether those orators were Balynt Zagoebel's corporals or Balynt Zagoebel himself. Standing on the lawn, on the gravel paths, laying waste to mounds of bushes and petunias, the crowd would attend a double spectacle organized in their honor. First panel of the diptych, the circus acts; second panel, the materialization between earth and sky, among the great spiders, of the best contemporary moralists. Through their ears, their eyes, their every pore, the crowd could slake both the thirst for entertainment and the desire for condemnation. The privileged—for here, too, some count as privileged—would spread out across the presently empty steps. From all of this, it seemed logical to assume that the concert was canceled. Just to be sure, I detached myself from the riveted community of onlookers, climbed up to the atrium, and searched for an open box office. Everything was closed, but there was a light on behind one shutter and I tapped my finger against the glass. After a long minute, I heard the sounds of conversation in an office I could not see, and then someone approached and removed the piece of cardboard that blocked the window. I recognized an administrator that I had met previously, I don't know where. Maybe he vaguely recognized me in turn; we greeted each other. No, the concert isn't canceled, he told me, with a bloodless voice that indicated unambiguously how little he adhered to Frondism, to Frondist principles, and, on this night especially, to Frondist notions of culture. The Djylas Quartet will perform as planned. Yes, they will play the works listed on the poster. I've had representatives of the authorities on the phone. Of all the authorities, he insisted. We will open the doors as usual, at seven thirty. The concert will be placed under the protection of security guards. At that moment a phone rang in the adjacent room. The man stood up again, nodded at me, wedged the cardboard barrier back into the window, and disappeared. The entryway was deserted. I remained there a few seconds. The idea of a concert needing official protection. The idea of an audience under threat, of musicians being subjected to such stupidity, to such fury. I returned to the staircase. The metamorphosis of the square was in progress. I consulted my watch. Five after seven. The sun still lit the chimney tops. Giant vertical banners hung without a wrinkle down the whole length of the buildings. In front of the steps, a truck maneuvered to stretch the acrobats' tightrope even tighter. On that part of the square, busy activity continued. It was clear, however, that soon everything would be complete, at the very moment that the doors were to spring apart for the Djylas enthusiasts. Before they could disappear into the atrium, they would experience the crushing weight of the Frondist ceremonial setting. There was still some hope that the masses would not yet have invaded the theater's front steps, for then those same enthusiasts would be forced to weave through the congregations of large and small collossi. They would have to open a path through thickets of citizens who were profoundly insulted that anyone could prefer Ichkouat's elegy for strings to the entertainment provided by the Party. No doubt, I reflected, this likely result had tickled the organizers' fancy. The discouragement would work, a natural sorting would occur. Only the most resolute men and women, those exasperated by Frondism and wanting to make their exasperation known, would have the audacity to brave the horde, its hostility barely mitigated by the presence of the civil guard. The evening was taking a very different turn from the fantasies I had so recently been nursing. I went down the stairs. I tried not to give in to despair, I tried not to suffocate in the poisonous atmosphere exuding from the spider symbols and flags. I tried to distract myself, to imagine myself elsewhere, with free lungs, inhaling a less tainted air than the air of Chamrouche. At the same time, I watched out for any individuals sidling toward me without bothering to give me a glance. I avoided two luxurious trench coats, skirted a bus full of militiamen that belched bitter smoke as it backed up onto the sidewalk. I got farther away. Three rowhouses separated me from Dojna's building. In the street, cars decked out in flags were revving up. Their purpose was to rally the masses, to invite them to the evening's glorious demonstration. From the croaks issuing from the loudspeakers, I learned that the event was called a rally-spectacular, and that it was set to begin at twenty hundred hours. The name Balynt Zagoebel was pronounced, but a motorcycle vroomed down the avenue at the same moment, so the meaning of the announcement escaped me. Perhaps they were promising the historic leader would give one of the speeches; or perhaps it was only an ideological reference that the militant had dropped into his microphone. The fading daylight persisted, tinting the silhouettes of the city, but I was too worried to draw any aesthetic pleasure from it. Instead I noted the raw cloudless sky, the absence of swallows. Despite the clement temperatures, springtime no longer worked its charm. Dojna let me in, superb and passionate as always, a queen whose power over me had not crumbled into routine or nostalgia. She had gotten a new hairstyle, medium length and extremely austere, a black frame around her face that did not hide her crow's feet nor the few wrinkles around her lips: marks of care, engravings of sensitivity and intelligence. Her eyes, the eyes of a painter, sparkled and smiled at me. She was wearing a low-cut dress in tones of gray and bronze, which we had chosen together in February and which suited her gorgeously. I must have had a strange look. She put her bare arm around me and pulled me into the entry, then toward an armchair. I stammered only a few inaudible words, my teeth chattering as if I'd been struck by a sudden attack of malaria. I drank tea and calmed down. Next we discussed. I summarized the situation. I did not declare any partiality to gratuitous heroics. I did not encourage Dojna to undergo the trial of immersion in the heart of the malevolent horde, which would already be packed into the stands and galvanized, already odious, already uncontrollable; I could not imagine our climbing toward the atrium between two rows of civil guards, under obnoxious jeers each one worse than the last and, why not, a few bursts of spittle. I feared, too, that the violence would overflow, all the way into the concert hall. If the security guards did not prove up to the task, nothing would prevent some vile attempt to silence the musicians, to extend, even into the theater itself, the triumph of racist diatribes and shouting, chanting, slogans. Incensed by the very concrete proximity of this threat, shocked as much as I was and more rebellious than I was, Dojna resolved to get ready right away. She wanted to be at the doors right when they opened. No, they won't impose their circus, their filthy festival, not on me, she raged. They won't condemn me to listening to their Zagoebel when I want to listen to a string quartet! Her cheeks were flushed. I've had enough of this nonsense, she protested. I watched her with tenderness. Moving among objects she had sculpted or painted, brushing against the mobiles and the photographic montages from her surrealist period, stopping near her recent canvases, before paintings I prized above all others—paintings I sometimes contemplated, that came to me in nostalgic moments, flaming landscapes in gray-blue or gray-green tones—pacing back and forth, proud and mutinous mistress of her personal worlds, and I knew how difficult they were to conquer, to discipline, to hold in place; I knew the secret codes, what haunted them. They won't keep me down, she said, with their idiotic jack-boot bullshit. I helped her slip on her coat, a darker bronze than her dress; even more than her magnificent raiment, it was her determination that decorated her, ennobled her. She grabbed her handbag, checked its contents, and closed it again with an energetic snap. I'm ready, she said. I advised her against bringing her starter pistol, a cheap contraption that she considered an indispensable weapon when she went out at night. That will only cause problems, I urged. If there's an incident with some idiots, it's better not to wave that thing around. She reflected, opened her bag, pulled the gun out, and sent it sliding down the entry table. It's true, we don't fight them here, she said regretfully. If we lived in the southern hemisphere, we'd be walking around with real guns in our pockets, and these lowlifes would hide in the walls. Let us picture the mythical pugnacity of the South, I said. The acts of resistance that are still possible, although less and less vigorous. Yes, Iakoub, let's picture it, she said. In the street, we walked without chatting. The neighborhood, not usually very lively at nightfall, was full of groups and wanderers. Echoes rumbled above Chamrouche, difficult to situate, difficult even to define. We arrived in view of the theater at twenty-five or twenty minutes to eight. The atmosphere had changed since I left. The preparatory phase had ended, and where the commotion of collective work had previously brightened the square with a little human note, now everything stood stagnant, a solid, terrifying façade without a single crack. Two immense white suns stared from either side, surrounded by dark red draperies striped with gray, their centers almost strangled by the symbol, powerful despite its deformity, anchored and glaring. All around, flags stretched from the mansard roofs down to the ground, with patterns identical to the main wall hangings. Black, white, burgundy, and gray. They had observed the principle of absolute symmetry. The resulting effect was to crush the individual and elevate the crowd. That crowd was dense and growing. The Party's security guards channeled the flood of sympathizers. They ensured its equal distribution, no doubt according to a plan made well in advance. Fantasy and improvisation counted for nothing among the values that sustained Frondism. The shuffling, stomping legions covered the square, but the theater staircase remained empty. A triple cordon of special troops in paramilitary uniforms were stationed on the first steps, cutting off access. More of these same robust individuals, visibly marked as elite members of the hygiene patrol, protected the space reserved for the circus performers: with trucks turned into platforms, a van serving as a common dressing room, all that equipment of dubious quality, and the tightrope, still somewhat slanted, stretched between a window and a lamppost. The government police were notable by their absence. I recalled the administrator's words. Guards would ensure the security of our concert. Now it became inescapably clear that this task had been confided to the henchmen of the troublemakers themselves. I squeezed Dojna's hand within my own. Our fingers were icy. For better or for worse, we were approaching the men in the special squad. They opened the links of their chain to allow us passage, without waiting for the explanations we had prepared on our way, the dreary justifications we were ready to offer. One disdainful glance from the wave's leader was all it took. The chain broke, and just as swiftly its links soldered back together. Several people had slipped in as we had, with no particular glory or humiliation. They climbed the stone steps. Therefore, it was not the Frondists' intention to block admission to the concert; they had only wanted to dissuade the less brave. Considering the obstacle course, the howling reception on the square and even on the avenue before that, it was a good bet that the concert hall would not be full. Dojna spoke this thought out loud. Once we had reached the columns of the atrium, we paused to look back. At our latitude, at that time of year, twilight comes quickly. The sun's glow was diminishing beyond the rooftops; soon the spotlights would come on and sweep their livid beams across the crowd, obliterating the last traces of individual awareness within them; then all would be ready for the glorification of leaders that would crown the thunderous Frondist festival. Thousands of disapproving eyes watched us from afar, from the square, from the sidewalks, but since the ceremony had not yet started, we were not forced to confront the hateful insult of their upraised arms, or some well-coordinated cascade of filth. At the foot of the stairs, the hollow island left for the circus marked a sort of sad, indifferent territory. Dojna asked me about the performers. They had an idle, fatalistic look, like animals in captivity. They waited patiently, sitting on whatever was convenient, or leaning against the vehicles that would soon substitute for the stage and backstage. They lacked enthusiasm, as Dojna observed. We decided to believe that they were there under duress. One might speculate about their participation in the rally, but all evidence suggested they did not enjoy the prospect of putting on this show, of going onstage beneath the banners and cheers of beasts. We knew very little about the marginal world of carnies, only a few vague ideas from literary references or childhood memory; nevertheless, we tended to imagine it as a liberated, anarchistic, fraternal world of hard work, in which the adherents of Balynt Zagoebel would be few. Only the name of the Vanzetti Circus told us anything; recently, out in the suburbs, I had noticed one of their simple posters, scribbled over with filthy epithets. Immediately we felt some sympathy for these inert musicians, these beaten-down dwarves, these acrobats and clowns chatting in small, bored circles; they, too, would have to demonstrate their talents in the shadows of uniforms and spidered armbands. They were not the ones who wished harm upon the Djylas Quartet. I could feel Dojna's anxiety as she pressed against me, despite her effort to feign calm. We were standing at the top of a slope, and the ascent had been difficult. More couples with tense looks and trembling lips, as well as a few isolated men, in evening dress or simpler outfits, continued to emerge from the crowd, to cross through the chains of security guards, and to climb slowly, as if in cinematic slow motion, up the steps. A spontaneous solidarity appeared instantly among these people. Without knowing each other, they sent greetings, quiet gestures devoid of emphasis, and reassuring smiles, even as, behind them, the storm was building. We entered the atrium, then the foyer. Everything was lit up as usual. The coatrooms were open, but in this uncertain, precarious situation, nobody wanted to check their things. Dojna, of course, did not leave her cape behind. She squeezed her black bag against her left hip as if it were a holstered revolver from the mythical South. As we entered the stalls she noticed some friends and went to greet them. I exchanged a few words with an amiable sexagenarian, who was tearing tickets without checking whether they were valid. He advised each arrival to pay no attention to the seat numbers. Everyone should sit in the stalls. There were no ushers this evening. Just before the doors opened, the employee told me, the Frondists had paid for three hundred seats, buying many more than the administration could or hoped to sell. So Balynt Zagoebel would do us the honor of coming in person, accompanied by his three hundred bodyguards. That surprising initiative cheered the ticket taker; he saw it as an excellent guarantee that the concert would go smoothly. As for myself, I did not know quite what to think, except that even the most beautiful passages from Tamian Ichkouat would hold no pleasure for me if I had to share oxygen with Balynt Zagoebel and his commandos while I listened. Everything was coming together to make this a terrible, nervous, and nerve-wracking evening. For the past hour, I felt, we had been moving blindly along a ravine, at the mercy of the slightest treacheries of the ground below. I joined Dojna and her friends: a gallery director who always seemed a bit too snobby for my taste; a rather awkward painter with a young woman, the model who lived with him; and Hakatia Badrinourbat. After a long time teaching at institutes in the provinces, beautiful Hakatia had returned to Chamrouche to direct a research laboratory. She had passed through my romantic existence in times that still burned in my memory like indulgent, faraway flames, much like my student years or my early, clumsy attempts to publish. If the marks left by our brief union now provoked nothing more than a sense of pleasant obsolescence, still they had not totally dissolved. Ever since we were twenty, some link had persisted between us. A conjunction of unavoidable circumstances had separated us, and then we no longer had any chance to see each other, but we never stopped corresponding, as if we were trying to revive here and there, in the course of our ever shorter letters, a very lazy game of seduction, as if always playing with the regret that we never lived, much more passionately, together. Now Hakatia was working in Chamrouche again. Since she was living without a companion, our friendship was at once restrained and slightly electrical. We saw each other very little, at her apartment or with Dojna, whom Hakatia liked; she had bought one of Dojna's blue-fire landscapes. I kissed Hakatia on the cheek and greeted the others. Our faces grew ever more somber at the rumors about the Frondists' musical delegation. We took our seats. We exchanged hypotheses. Three hundred brown brains touched by sudden musical grace: an unlikely miracle in which we had no faith, not even for a second. In this setting, an invasion by fanatics would constitute sabotage on a grand scale. But there was that transaction, that enormous sum the Party had disbursed to gain legal access to the concert hall. Three hundred seats paid for, to the last penny, the optimistic sexagenarian had said. Certain of the trench coats' behaviors followed a psychology that was, to us, opaque. Perhaps the money that gushed through the Party coffers encouraged a taste for irrational pomp. Perhaps the Party's first delirious tendencies were complicated by an ancient, unquenched thirst for bourgeois respectability. Consciousness of limitless power and too-easy impunity might also provoke a vicious cynicism, a new kind of perversion: not content to humiliate his victim through violence, the criminal adds an outrageous mockery, a second humiliation consisting of compensation. In both cases, no doubt, the Frondists found an acute pleasure. Then I ceased to speculate on the subject; it felt like stirring a fetid swamp. Echoes from outside vibrated around us, though stifled here, at a distance. We were sitting inside a precious jewel box of a space, and, within our velvet casing, two full centuries late to the story, we had the impression that something of our cultural integrity had been preserved. We felt no great admiration for the gilding or sentimentality; nothing fascinated us about the society—happily dead and buried—of little lords and ladies. But now I contemplated the overdecorated moldings, the old-fashioned ornamentation, the baroque scrolls, the pastoral scenes so totally detached from contemporary reality that their improbability came to bear a message. I took a deep breath, un-nerved by the rumbles we could hear from outside, yet indecisive, because the luster and curves of the architecture dimmed the credibility of our fears. Dojna leaned against my shoulder. In return I slumped back a bit against her. I avoided touching her forearm, brushing her bare skin with my hand. Anxiety had transformed my fingers into glacial objects, and I did not wish to inflict contact with them upon her. More people were arriving in small groups, passing through the crushed-velvet curtains behind us. They filled the stalls without regard to seat numbers. They left not a single seat unoccupied between themselves and their neighbors, contrary to the usual misanthropic reflex of independence. Already it was clear that the expectation of musical enjoyment played only a secondary role in our obstinate congregation, gathering close together rather than running away as fast as our legs could carry us. At that moment, a loudspeaker shouted a slogan over the square and the crowd took it up, chanting with fast-growing fervor. It was ten minutes to eight and the stalls continued to fill. This audience did not include the sorts of people who attend gala receptions. One would have to characterize it as the more varied clientele of matinees: gray-haired professors, very few young people, women in heavy makeup, intellectual women both pretty and plain, a few single people in slightly eccentric or worn-out jackets, some students from the Conservatory. At the far end of one row, three men were sitting in silence, visibly intimidated by all the gilding and crystal, the beribboned lambs and shepherds, the soft seats. They wore modest work shirts with broad stripes; their discomfort showed that they belonged neither to the stage crew nor to the first wave of the avalanche we feared would crash down upon us. One of them turned: a large, dark man, blessed with a rustic face and an unforgettable gaze that bewitched with a single captivating green flash. Outside, a new round of vociferation burst out, its phrases chopped through the microphones and taken up by the choir in enthusiastic fragments and amplified clamor, all expertly orchestrated with that knowledge of escalation that all ring-leaders possess—that exact science of the collective mood, that art. The roar ebbed and flowed without end. It turned out to be less thunderous than expected: the atrium's columns must have broken the waves of sound, scattered them under the vaulted ceiling in the foyer, muted them among the curtains of the arcade. When the doors closed and the dam of wall hangings fell again, the concert might enjoy a real, however derisory, quiet. Beyond that, there was no sense in holding out any such hope. Under the effect of the con-flagration beginning outside, nobody could have much faith in the immediate future. A heavy web had descended upon us, sticky and dense; and in one corner of that web, ready for action, the Frondist spider was stirring. Mute with apprehension in our seats, we moved less and less. The spectators all sat stiff-necked. They looked straight ahead. House lights brightened the stage. The wings, in contrast, seemed shadowy; not a soul. The music stands stood like abstract sculptures in front of the four straight chairs, not very comfortable ones by the look of them. We stared at all this, petrified, our rigidity as excessive as the stiff gestures of the three workmen. It was eight o'clock. Out there, something had changed. Thousands of chests exhaled a terrifying ovation, and at almost the same instant we heard the sound of shoes and voices resonating through the foyer. Balynt Zagoebel was on schedule, then. I forced myself to show no interest, no reaction, no awareness, not even a random gleam from my eyes as he and his men entered the theater. Intoxicated by acclamation, he had just mounted an assault on the theater in the company of his shock troops, as if this were a military objective. I did not want to participate, through my attitude, in his victory. Dojna did not turn her head toward the back either. Both friends and strangers nearby had adopted a similar line of conduct. We had no means at our disposal to show the Frondists the contempt that their machinations and their philosophy deserved, to remind them that, here, the center of attention was the stage, the music, the musicians, and not the supposedly music-loving special forces with their khaki ideology, their deformed, bristling, brownish ideology. I had slid my right arm under Dojna's cape. We were both trembling, overcome with indignation, a mixture of fury and fear. The surge of uniforms felt like a moral blow, but even more bruising was our very poor apprehension of what those uniforms might have in mind. In the galleries a tumult swelled, imitating euphoria. With a laughing nonchalance, the militants distributed themselves around the parterre, occupied the boxes and the balconies. I expected one of their shameful banners to unfurl from the nosebleeds, but nothing of the sort occurred: only their arrival in a disruptive troop, although they were orderly enough that after only a few brief minutes they had succeeded in filling all the seats in the room. I have never been good at estimating the size of groups, but it seems to me that they surpassed the already considerable number of three hundred. Amidst all the confusion, the lateral chandeliers darkened and the footlights came on, along with the spotlights from the loft. The musicians came to arrange their instruments and their sheet music. They did not even glance at the audience, whose rumblings announced no real welcome but rather the raw excitement that precedes a boxing match. They won't be able to play, Dojna whispered sorrowfully. No, they won't be allowed to play, was my own thought. We felt wholehearted compassion for the members of the quartet. Their names echoed mechanically along the edges of my memory. Mourtaza Tchopalav, Ansaf Vildan, Dimirtchi Makionian, and Tchaki Estherkhan, the viola player. It took a heroic amount of courage to be there, to tolerate confrontation with such an audience. To accept the idea that, soon, they would have to take the instruments back out of their cases, check the tuning, and, with a firm bow, without showing the unhealthy dread that had taken the place of ordinary stage fright, attack the first measure of the first piece. Tchopalav, Vildan, Dimirtchi Makionian, and Tchaki Estherkhan went back into the wings. We had not applauded to greet their transitory apparition. To the left of the parterre, however, some joke triggered a gust of laughter, soon amplified by a cascade of revolting jeers and a bantering exchange between one end of the room and the other. Then all fell silent, suddenly, as if following an order. Then I noticed, standing in a box next to the place of honor, the mediocre movie star from the '40s and '50s, the eternal B-movie supporting actor, in whom so many now recognized their pharmacist, their butcher, their leader. Energetic, conquering, and severe, Balynt Zagoebel gazed out over his troops. A few men accompanied him, packed into light-beige or gray leather coats. One of the acolytes must have given the signal for quiet. There was a long, surprisingly calm pause. The special squads no longer chattered, meditated, or dozed, avoiding any notice of our presence. Balynt Zagoebel fell back into the half-shadows of his box; his entourage sat down, except for a bodyguard who remained planted near a stylized bouquet of ferns with the expression of a sentinel granted the right to kill without warning. Still the Frondists did not reveal their intentions. Since the concert hall was now full, the upholstered doors and curtains closed, so that the sounds from the rally-spectacular decreased, reduced to zero, or almost. There. We found ourselves locked in, sharing our living space with an army of brutes whose plans we could not manage to figure out, for anything was imaginable other than the lack of a plan. This disciplined, arrogant truce was part of an inexorable series of tactical moves. Now the light from the central chandelier dimmed. The decisive phase of the concert would no longer be deferred. Pastoral paintings of ruddy-cheeked shepherds and marquises in disguise faded into nothingness. Out of the darkness, the stage alone emerged, with its music stands, its chairs and open instrument cases, the cello already out of its bag and resting at a slant in the place where Dimirtchi Makionian would soon sit and play. Around Dojna and me, the two or three hundred people not in uniform steeled themselves for disaster. I could make out the spectators' shapes. Necks retracted between shoulders, as if the ceiling plaster were threatening to crumble and fall like rain. On my right I could hear Dojna's halting breath, and, at my left, the art dealer's short, strange gasp. A little farther on, Hakatia let out a sigh. She was holding her neighbor's hand. Our weakness, our stubbornness, our disgust, our pride, our valor. We busied ourselves with examining the chrome-plated clips that pinched the sheet music, or scrutinizing the cello, the curve of its soundboard, the blackness of its fingerboard and tuning pegs. Then the members of the quartet came forward. We applauded them generously. My vision was blurred with tears, I feel no shame in admitting that. Stifled sobs and clapping hands were all we had to offer them as a defense against the malevolent pressure of Zagoebel and his gang. And this: finally making a gesture, no matter how conventional, delivered us a little from the stagnant nightmare into which we had been sinking, until then, without a struggle. Among the Frondist ranks, the khaki shirts and spider armbands remained still as marble. It's awful, I don't understand what they want, Dojna murmured. I don't understand either, I said. But we would soon find out. The artists concentrated a few seconds, watching the bow of the first violin, Ansaf Vildan, from the corners of their eyes, and then, with a single sweeping movement, they launched into the beginning of Naïsso Baldakchan's third quartet. For the last time that night, I checked my watch: it showed seventeen minutes after eight. The musicians played amidst a silence for which none of us had dared hope. After a moment's uncertainty they seemed reassured and threw themselves deep into the world of music. And yet I could feel that this intense peace would not last. The hall was quiet, the shadowy zones divided into blocs of apprehension or hostility. It was impossible to believe that the Frondists would listen with reverence to the music of an immigrant composer, one so repulsed by bellicosity and lies that he'd thrown himself under a train, so nauseated by the humanist lectures of the war criminals at work in Chamrouche that before going to his death, he pinned to his sweater this very explicit request: I beg you, do not bury me with representatives of the human race. I thought of Naïsso Baldakchan's bitter fate, his failed exile, and that mangled body that the authorities had, as their form of tribute, hastily trashed in a mass grave. I did not enjoy the music at all. My anxiety had not been tempered by the velveted atmosphere that now reigned in the theater. And then the velvet caved in, the atmosphere tore apart. Just as Dimirtchi Makionian's cello took up the rippling theme that the violins and the viola had just introduced, a loud voice crowed from the box where Balynt Zagoebel was lurking. What a bore! What is it, anyway? the voice protested. You're not telling me that's music, are you? Who wrote it, eh? Who hatched that shitty little egg? The answer burst from the shadows of the second-floor balcony. It's Baldakoochian! The Frondists guffawed, roaring with full-throated glee. Bal-da-cooch-i-an! Bal-da-cooch-i-an! a small group began to chant, and all those music-loving uniforms on the floor, all those well-built and ebullient representatives of Frondist health repeated the syllables with impeccable discipline. What a bunch of bastards, what bastards, Dojna sobbed. She hunted for a tissue in her bag. I remembered the starter pistol she had agreed to leave behind. And her comments about the cities in the South as we imagined them, their permanent insurrection, their inflexible guerilla fighters. Dojna Magidjamalian: I imagined her in another context, drawing a heavy revolver out of its hiding place, but at the last second, hesitating to shoot because of the darkness, unable to resolve to aim into darkness, hesitating, seized by scruples, halted by her intelligence and sensibility, unable to master the necessary culture of killing, ashamed of the willingness or ability to kill or injure at random, hesitating to fire her weapon in the barbarians' direction. Just as shocked as she was, I gasped—suffocation, a physical symptom of defeat. Onstage, the quartet had stopped playing. The bows' tips brushed the floorboards. Finished, yes, the concert was finished. We had tried our best, we had assembled our pitiful energies against the boycotters, but the time had come to drop our weapons. Suddenly calm returned, an absolute calm, and Balynt Zagoebel's team leaned over the ledge of their box. A '40s trench coat barked across to the artists. The dismayed musicians seemed to have trouble regaining their composure. They blinked, like people emerging from a very bad dream and realizing that the night surrounding them remains full of danger. That's enough Baldakshin! the trench coat proclaimed. We want music for the people! Fun music, good music! Intellectuals in penguin suits don't know how to entertain the people! It's popular culture we want, not the high culture of Baldakshit and company. Baldakshit? No, thank you! And for a full minute the jubilant hall hammered out: Bal-dak-shit! Bal-dak-shit! Then another of the corporals imposed a new silence on this commotion. Their ability to obtain immediate quiet proved there was nothing spontaneous about those chants. The members of the Djylas Quartet had gotten up and closed their sheet music. Tchaki Estherkhan was returning her viola to its case. I don't recall exactly when I moved, but we were standing, too, stunned with indignation and sorrow. For a few seconds nothing happened. Without any special effort, we could make out thumping music on the square, the simple rhythm of a bass drum: outside, the circus must have been in full swing. Then Balynt Zagoebel appeared and swaggered out, although there was no spotlight trained on him. He was accustomed to grandstands and endowed with a stentorian voice. What's this, now? You're not about to fly out from under our noses like a flock of finches, are you? No, out of the question! We paid for a full show! These good people paid, and not chicken feed, either! The militants were bent double with mirth. Any reference to birds had a disgusting way of tickling them, and Balynt Zagoebel had just extended his lips by three millimeters at each corner, granting his troops permission to laugh. Sit down! Everyone sit back down! The musicians will fly back to their filthy nests and tweet out a little dance for us. Come, madame, come, gentlemen, play a nice song for the people! Pluck a little passaquailia! Show a little spirit, for God's sake! Show your fans you're not a bunch of wet hens! The room cackled. Very pale and very beautiful under the spotlights, Tchaki Estherkhan closed her viola case. The violinists followed suit. The cellist, Dimirtchi Makionian, who had not brought the voluminous case or protective bag for his instrument onto the stage, waited for his comrades to leave. There was some agitation on the floor. Fifteen men dressed in black came jogging down the left-hand aisle. They bounded nimbly onto the stage. Flexible tactical shoes, military coveralls, the special symbol of an elite unit on their armbands. They formed a half-circle behind the artists. More henchmen in dark gray shirts had followed and now veered toward the wings to neutralize the stage manager and the electrical technicians. These were actual military maneuvers being performed in the theater now. The dim lighting did not stop the machine from functioning, no cog jammed to sabotage it. Just like the musicians, the audience was surrounded, caught in a trap. After exchanging a look with his leader, one man detached himself from the group in position around the quartet. The coverall rendered him an anonymous silhouette. And yet, there was some indefinable difference between him and the others who encouraged his advance. He approached Tchaki Estherkhan, one arm reaching out halfway, the hand open, as if approaching an animal that he was taming. Assurance emanated from his posture, an assurance that was nothing like crude Frondist disdain. His movements were fluid, as if suffused with certainty: he would succeed in melting any vague desire the young woman might feel to revolt; as soon as he could touch her hair, she would warm to him, calm down, obey. Come on, he was saying. Take out your violin. Don't be afraid. He was not threatening her, not at all. His inspiration must have come from a habit of dazzling success, in dance clubs or elsewhere. Won't you give us the pleasure, he was saying. But his hand was circling at the height of a horse's muzzle, as if he were speaking not to a woman but to a frightened filly. Come on, give us this pleasure, he insisted. His cajoling echoed, carried by the acoustics of the space. Suddenly, as Tchaki Estherkhan seemed not to succumb to his fascination, he turned toward his leader, and I could see him better. He had the same green eyes as the workman with the two friends, who had looked so lost, a short time ago, among the gilding and velvet. At the second this realization occurred to me, I saw that exact young man walking with quick steps up the aisle, crossing the footlights, and taking a stance before the audience. The Frondist ranks buzzed. This figure springing out of the shadows must not have been listed on their program. While his two companions climbed without haste through the side entrance onto the stage, the young man addressed the seducer who had confused violin and viola, filly and woman. Strangely, that seducer radiated joy. Matko! I can't believe it! he exclaimed. Bieno! the other snarled in response. Bieno, you piece of shit! And he slapped him with all his strength. Our tragic reflex was to applaud this spectacular gesture. No doubt, sooner or later, some incident would have lit the fuse. The man named Bieno did not strike back. He did not rub his cheek. A childish stupefaction had softened his features. He stood immobile, seeking to decode something in his adversary's gaze. During this time, the head of the elite unit dug under his jacket. He aimed a gun and calmly shot two bullets at the man who had struck one of his soldiers. Our applause stopped cold. A young woman's piercing shriek ripped the air apart, and no doubt other cries burst out here and there, wails of horror, but the thunder of Frondist ovation covered them all. Tchaki Estherkhan had fallen back. Dimirtchi Makionian had left his cello lying on the floor. Now a music stand and a chair lay fallen. The armbands with special spiders had drawn away, but still they blocked the musicians' retreat into the wings. The Djylas Quartet constituted a compact and miserable little troop. To the right, clear and bright in the footlights, the injured man twisted with effort, crawling toward the cello. His comrades wavered downstage, unsure what to do. One of them had the musculature of a weightlifter, with a bull's neck and enormous fists; the other had a scruffy, pathetic look, the mask of a panic-stricken bird. In the stalls, everyone was paralyzed with shock. But, predictably, after that minute of fear came a wave of panic. I imagined our fragility, Dojna's fragility, and the trampled cadavers that inevitably turn up after a stampede caused by terror. I wrapped my arm around Dojna.

Listen, I said. If people rush for the exit, let's not get caught up with them. Let's stay together. The torrent of Frondist applause was petering out. The smell of burnt gunpowder stung my nostrils. I could hear the thugs out on the walkway, obstructing the departure of people trying to flood outside. The security guards had control of the exits and they had decided not to open the trap, not yet. Their methods proved effective enough to overcome all confusion in a few seconds. Silence fell again. Gazes converged either toward the stage or toward Balynt Zagoebel's box, according to disposition. We could hear a trumpet, some cymbals, out on the street. We could hear, too, the wet croak of the injured man, who was stretched out near the cello, but unable to get his hand on it. The hero of fillies contemplated him with mouth agape, sinking into total stupefaction. Two gray shirts evacuated him from the spotlit circle. The wrestler turned to the right, to the left, with an air of perplexity. The cellist stepped forward and touched his arm, as if inviting him to join the unhappy family of musicians. The bird was crouched over the dying man, and I caught another glimpse of those superb eyes, misted now with tears, or perhaps already pale with death. The bird squeezed his companion's hand with awkward sorrow. The cellist was moving to offer help when two commando coveralls cut in front of him. They lifted the bird up by the shoulders. The Frondists were overjoyed at catching one of their prey, and such a typical specimen, the exact target of their xenophobic fetish since time immemorial. They tore the sleeve off the bird's shirt to reveal the evidence, the black down covering

his skin. Jeers and insults roared through the theater. The bird struggled between the two men, who were twisting his wrists. The wrestler walked up to them and, without warning, loosed his arm like a
catapult. The arm twister on the right fell, knocked flat, his knees
giving way. The second dropped his grip and initiated a tactical retreat in the direction of his peers, but he had no time to evade the
incoming blow, a fantastic punch below the jaw. He crumpled immediately, tripping over the cello and knocking over chairs. The
wrestler seemed entirely disposed to continue in the same manner.
Already he was stepping over the cello's neck, approaching a third
coverall. Then there was another detonation, and that man, so full of
power and courage, attempted a feeble gesture, then gave up on wiping his burst-open forehead, and collapsed backwards, with stiff legs.
The Frondists shoved back the musicians, who were trying to flee
into the wings. The group leader had reholstered his weapon. He
tugged the zipper on his jacket closed. The room stank of gunpowder and murder. Someone had caught the bird again. The bird was
trying to get away. He was thrashing and writhing in a useless, jerky
manner, and instinctively everyone quieted in order to hear what he
was shouting, his unbearable, rasping voice cracked with emotion
and fear. My name is Aram Bouderbichvili, he shouted, between
terrible sobs. Aram Bouderbichvili. That name should mean something to you—doesn't that name mean anything to you? At this,
Balynt Zagoebel leaned over his box ledge and gave a signal. The
central chandelier came back on, flooding the theater with a false

daylight, which had the sole merit of bringing us abruptly among the victims, after that moment of abomination when we had been silent observers. Now that the entire room was lit, our situation as hostages became more evident. Our role was not limited to remaining upright and facing the stage. We were not simply witnesses; we had been assigned another purpose in this tragedy. Untouched by events, the smiling, painted marquises armed with spinning wheels and delicate skeins, the aristocratic shepherds examined us from their woodland groves. The shirts raised their heads toward their leader. Good. Very good, that leader approved. Finally, a show that the masses can enjoy. Actions, reactions! An exciting little squabble! After the string quartet, a feather trio! Very edifying! But this gilded cage isn't comfortable for the people. It's not an appropriate place for healthy entertainment. Time for a change of scene! And there's another show outside, anyway. Why have two shows at the same time? We've already said it, we've repeated it like parrots: one people, one culture! But lessons have a hard time penetrating some skulls. As for us, we'll always support popular culture, always and forever. Come, let's bring these ladies and gentlemen outside. I reproached myself sharply for dragging Dojna into an ambush. Earlier, in her apartment, I should have persuaded her not to get mixed up in this. What now? she asked. Now, I whispered, we will leave under close escort. We will be shoved, and insulted, and when we make our way through their much-vaunted popular culture, they will throw rotten eggs at us, they will spit on us, they will assault us. And then, we will go up to your apartment to wash it all off and take care of each other. The curtain will fall on this evening. And whatever can heal in us will begin to form scars. Keep hold of me. Whatever happens, we're together. Our legs felt like cotton. Khaki shirts, grays, browns, blacks, were organizing the evacuation. Shoved by the black coveralls, the members of the Djylas Quartet had been forced to jump down over the footlights and joined us in the aisle. We were already on the way to the exit, and nobody looked back at the stage; none of us wanted to look back at the stage, where four brutes were using the two violins, the viola, and the cello to pummel the two prone dead workers. Dimirtchi Makionian and Ansaf Vildan, the first violin, were supporting Tchaki Estherkhan as she walked. She did not hold back her tears, but despite them she had not lost her dignity. Howls and orders swelled from all around us. Those barks, marking the cadence of our slow, our sheeplike progression toward the foyer, managed to distract me from my fear. Dojna clung to me tightly, and I realized that, with an instinctive gesture, I had just grabbed the elbow of the gallery director. I felt ashamed and let go; then it was he who put his arm under mine. He was holding Hakatia Badrinourbat close. We formed a sort of stricken chain. We got to the arcade, then the foyer. Young thugs in armbands guided us toward the doors with growing impatience. When we emerged from the atrium, an enormous uproar surrounded us: the crowd was welcoming their triumphant heroes, whose exploit consisted of bringing the intellectuals onto the circus steps. The crowd was warmed up, red hot. Spotlights swept back and forth across them, excited them. The sky above was dark as tar. A battery of floodlights, aimed toward the ground, sprayed across the areas not open to the public. Powerful beacon lights marked the theater columns and blinded us, and then illuminated the grand staircase, still empty, where the security guards were directing us. The steps, with tight spotlights sweeping back and forth, became a second stage for the rally-spectacular. The first act, carnies performing under duress; and now, onto the brilliantly lit stone, came this new attraction: the lovers of suspect music, those who compromised themselves with neg artists, who sympathized with the enemy, with flea-bitten chickens from the South, and who were now to be publicly reeducated with all swiftness. The leathers and paramilitary shirts began an arbitrary triage, picking through our troop to delegate three or four privileged rows who would remain at the center of the lights. Their gestures were stripped of all diplomacy. In the free air, spurred onward by the shouting thousands, Frondism could be expressed more easily, more naturally. Shoves and blows accompanied that expeditious minute. A menacing cordon threw us stumbling down to the middle of the staircase. Dojna was still with me. We had gotten separated from Hakatia Badrinourbat and the painter, and from the two violinists, Mourtaza Tchopalav and Ansaf Vildan. Along with the majority of people the armbands had expelled from the theater, they had been told to get down off the stairs and to run to the borders of the square. Two rows of slant-armed salutes marked their path. The jeering crowd closed in on them. Incessant screeches pierced our ears. I saw Balynt Zag-oebel on a balcony, in a halo of white suns, flanked by inky spiders, and whooping in unison with the masses. Several Balynt Zagoebels at the same time, then, were assuming the role of orchestrator of popular instincts, supreme leader over the death throes of Cham-rouche. They were identical in their physical appearance, and their speech, too, was unaltered, despite traveling between the parallel bodies that the ubiquitous director borrowed in order to manifest. One people, Balynt Zagoebel cawed into the microphone, while behind us another Balynt Zagoebel was inspecting the deserted concert hall with his general staff. One people, one culture, one show! he squawked. Once we were packed into the center of the staircase, the Frondists fell away. They surrounded us, watching us from the edge of the columns, but from a distance we must have looked like we were huddling close together by choice, like a small quarantine of fearful animals. We trembled, blinking our eyes under the ferocious spotlights' attack. The people want culture, not avicul-ture! Zagoebel went on honking. Not this Baldak-bullshit for feather-brained intellectuals and pretentious peacocks! Not this de-generate art for chickenshits! The crowd reacted to each vague state-ment with fanatical yells. The speaker used the time to flip through the spiral notebook where he had written down his lines. For too long these intellectuals have taken the people for pigeons! he rasped, exasperated. These little doves of decadence! The people don't need some parrot telling them what they should or shouldn't peck at! The people love clowns, they love acrobats! The leader's words unleashed eruptions of rabid cheers that echoed between the buildings. One word was all it would take to begin the lynching of enemies, the massacre of the final symbolic square of internal foreigners, the tearing apart of our pitiful little pack. When Balynt Zagoebel added nothing more, the circus acts began again. Trumpet and tuba played traditional melodies from festival music. In protest against the threats hanging over them, the band played horribly, a jumble of false notes. A tiny woman, a dwarf, had been forced to sit on the windowsill at one end of the tightrope. Her legs hung in the void, and the bodyguards who were dandling her made it obvious that they intended to throw her down to the sidewalk if the circus performers refused to cooperate. The vantage point we occupied was ideal, the best view in the entire square. A clown twirled in the space cleared for the acrobats. He climbed onto the roof of a truck, climbed back down, ran around on the blacktop, loomed on the roof of the vehicle serving as the band's platform, slid back down to the ground after wobbling dizzily on the hood or a ladder. He mimed wild panic, along with his desire to break the ring of security guards. He brandished a sort of cardboard axe as he stood a grotesque watch, provoking general hilarity. As soon as he approached the Frondists close enough to yell at them, they threw him violently back to centerstage, under the tightrope and the acid floodlights. There he pirouetted, rolled, gathered his wits, continued his restless zigzags. Near the lamppost, where the tightrope ended, lay several

bodies. Occasionally the clown would trot right up to that impro-
vised morgue. Then he raised his axe in a gesture of terror and fled,
confronting the Frondist rampart with buffoonish taunts, attacking
it only to be swiftly disarmed and tossed back into the light. Not a
second's pause interrupted this monstrous ballet that so delighted
the crowd. Even in the farthest rows, the nosebleed seats where nobody could see anything, they screamed with contagious laughter.
Then the snare drum rolled out a signal: the game was about to get
more interesting. In the window, next to the dwarf in her spangled
jumpsuit, there was an increased commotion. The clown hoisted
himself onto the roof of the van closest to the lamppost. He looked
toward the second floor and, slowly, his shoulders shaking with sobs,
he knelt. Up there, two trench coats had burst out of the apartment's
shadows to tackle a tightrope walker who was refusing their exhor-
tations. It was not a fair fight. The goal was to force the reluctant funambulist out onto the narrow ledge, beyond which roared an abyss.
One way or another, the trench coats succeeded. Eyes smarting from
the spotlights' beams, dizzied by the Frondists' practiced blows, a
being who looked nothing like an acrobat stood sputtering, wiping
a hand over his mouth and rubbing his left shoulder, waiting for
what came next. A piece of string cinched his beggar's overcoat tight
at the waist. With remarkable timing, Balynt Zagoebel's voice rang
out in the loudspeakers: We support the people, but we do not support birds! We'll ruffle their feathers every time! Well, too bad for
them! If they don't fly away, they deserve it! On the second story, the

confused struggle started up again. It involved two punching bags. The child-sized woman, forbidden to cover her face, forced to remain seated with her eyes open wide before the crime. And the bird, dressed like a bum from the poor countries. The trench coats were battering him with punches, pushing him toward the tightrope. The street! Balynt Zagoebel trumpeted. The street has its own methods, good old popular methods, handed down for a thousand years! And they'll be good for another thousand years! Thanks to all of us! The street doesn't waste time on flighty talk! This isn't some kind of cuckoo committee! If there's a migration problem to deal with, the street deals with it! At the corner of the building, the Frondists had propelled their victim expertly, and now he wavered above the void, advancing with small, uncertain steps, his arms stretched out in a cross. The square howled. Ironic encouragement punctuated his every hesitation. Again the clown was standing on the roof of the van. In alignment with the tightrope, he swung his axe in one direction and the other, in a careful parody of the bird's movements, as if he hoped this would help the bird keep his balance. Everyone gets their chance! In the right circumstances, the jitters can give you wings! Balynt Zagoebel announced. Then, suddenly, the amateur funambulist toppled and crashed seven or eight meters below. The band had been pausing frequently, as if exhausted. Now again they stopped, but an armband-shirt leaned into the percussionist's ear and the musicians looked up toward the dwarf; the laughing armband-shirts were grabbing her under her arms and tossing her back and forth.

The bass drum began once again to choke out the nightmarish time. The clown had jumped down to the pavement. He shook with grief over the broken body. After a few moments' prostration, he dragged it toward the pile where the others lay, then he jabbed his fists toward the barrier of special troops. The uniforms sent him rolling back to the lamppost again. The ecstatic crowd began to sing: He's one of your bro-o-others! Dropped in the dirt like the o-o-others! The clown screamed something indistinct in the direction of the spider-symbols, the audience, the flags. You can't make an omelette without breaking a few eggs! Balynt Zagoebel philosophized. Wild with excitement, the crowd chanted: Who's up next! Who's up next! There. We had to witness several martyrdoms in succession. The idea of escape from this spectacle was as ridiculous as the clown's comings and goings, the mummeries he added to death. We could not get away. A human rampart surrounded the enclosure where Frondism forced us to contemplate, passively, the unacceptable. Immobile, instinctively pressed close together, our only recourse was to squint our eyes shut or to cry. But even if tears dissolved the outlines, they did not modify the horror, what it was, its nature. All that remained to us was the solitude of hands clutching other hands. Next to me stood Dojna and the art dealer, Dimirtchi Makionian, the cellist, and Tchaki Estherkhan, the viola player. Tchaki Estherkhan was trembling like a leaf. Dojna had taken hold of her wrist and consoled her now and then with a furtive, inaudible word. We did not speak. We communicated only through basic physical contact, through the harmony of our quivering and catching breath. The tumult was reaching proportions difficult to describe, with sudden, empty pauses, evil silences soon submerged in another cresting wave. Birds appeared on the second story, made a few steps on the tightrope, fell, died. One of them was stubborn and denied his identity. I would have recognized him anyway, because of his shirt with the sleeve torn off. My name is Aram Bouderbichvili! he proclaimed as he struggled on the window ledge. Does that name mean anything to you? Does that name mean anything to you? Then the floodlights that shone on the circus floor went out, and the spotlights swung to the central part of the staircase, to us. Now our group became a new target, designated by Balynt Zagoebel for the people of Chamrouche. A vast expanse of white steps stretched between us and the first chains of security guards. The crowd booed us without even a pause for breath. Perhaps, at that moment, we should have initiated some sort of contrite, apologetic retreat, hanging our heads and groveling to those who were castigating us; we should have demonstrated that we finally understood the extent of our aesthetic and sentimental errors, the righteousness of their popular indignation, the healthy vigor of bigotry and racism. Perhaps, in that deafening minute, with humility, we could have forced open the walls of the trap. Perhaps we could have passed through, retreated under the rows and squirts of saliva, pursued by Balynt Zagoebel's final diatribe, his stale, hackneyed jokes that he had recycled a hundred times, about stuffed turkeys and wet hens, about intellectuals who could spend a whole night discussing the sex lives of chicka-dees. Perhaps. But we remained inert, bereft of initiative, fixed before the ocean of insults and crime, and this was received, by the most hardened among them, as a concerted expression of defiance. That's why two grenades were thrown at us. The first one exploded at our backs, where it had been thrown from the atrium. Instantly the det-onation dispersed everything around me. The blast deafened me and, in a paradoxical absence of noise, I saw dark debris floating at human height, the debris of bodies. Then I was knocked over and trampled, I don't know by whom. Dojna was no longer at my side. I slid forward. Someone stepped on my leg again, then on my neck. I was losing blood. I had the impression that many of us were lying there bleeding on the steps, but in fact most were uninjured and scattering, screaming. The security guards did not open ranks to let them leave. My vision was clouding. The second grenade bounced on the steps and landed at Dojna's feet. At that moment several peo-ple were stumbling or crawling next to her. Tchaki Estherkhan had fallen and was trying to regain her balance, clinging to Dojna's bronze-tinted cape. The cape was stained with blood. Dojna bent down and took up the grenade. She held it in her hand. There were people all around her and the Frondists seemed too far away. She hesitated to throw the object back at those uniforms. She hesitated. Dojna. Dojna Magidjamalian.

To her memory, I dedicate this text.

THIS IS THE STORY OF A WRITER AND A CELLIST. They met in the hospital, where they were lying side by side, after a Frondist attack. They are released on the same day. The cellist has lost two fingers on his right hand. He can still hold a bow, but he has also received a nasty injury to his left shoulder, and the surgeons have advised him to wait at least three months before playing his instrument again. His arm hangs, painful and swollen, like a wing with severed joints. The writer, Iakoub Khadjbakiro, has undergone surgery on his legs, but, even worse, his eyes are damaged. His vision is declining and very rudimentary at present, reduced to a colorless haze; in a few months, even this precarious perception of forms will be taken away from him. He knows that he will write no more. Other writers dictate their works after going blind, but he no longer has any desire to write books.

The writer and Dimirtchi Makionian, the cellist, cross the threshold of the hospital, and a doctor shakes their hands and jokes: Out you go now! We've seen enough of you here! But abruptly he realizes that this is not a polite thing to say to a man threatened by blindness, and he abandons the two of them. Actually, the three. Accompanying them is the writer's friend, Hakatia Badrinourbat. She has offered to let them stay with her for at least a week: time for them to rediscover a world beyond the realms of treatment rooms, bandage rooms, anesthetic rooms; time for both of them to prepare for their future solitude.

They arrive at her apartment in a cab. She lives in a new neighborhood, on the eighth floor of a building with modern architecture in concrete and bluish glass. Iakoub Khadjbakiro can distinguish only an imposing, nebulous, muddled mass, for the sky reflects on it, as it does on the mirrored walls of neighboring buildings.

They say almost nothing. Hakatia Badrinourbat is a discreet woman, good at remaining quiet when her companions need silence. Iakoub Khadjbakiro thinks about all that he might yet have written and that he will no longer write; he thinks about the blue sky that today he confuses with walls; he thinks about the button panel on the elevator, whose numbers he cannot read. He thinks about the lamentable present, about the crippled future, but not about the past. Dimirtchi Makionian smiles at Hakatia, several times, in a distracted manner. He barely knows her. He accepted her invitation, her kindness, her consideration. But he has no idea where it will lead him. The idea of what path he might follow from here does not concern him, or sometimes it squeezes his heart, but as if he were already very far from his point of departure, already on his way.

Hakatia Badrinourbat opens the door of her large, bright, comfortable apartment. She shows the two men to their bedrooms. There are flowers in each, and clothes that belong to them, objects that are still dear to them. Hakatia is intervening here as the final link in a long chain of solidarity and friendship. Many have contributed to putting this haven together. Hakatia's home was chosen through a collective decision as much as an individual initiative. Behind Hakatia's generosity and kindness there is Ansaf Vildan, Mourtaza Tchopalav, the director of an art gallery, painters, models, musicians, and anonymous others.

The writer and the cellist take possession of their rooms slowly, with humility and emotion. Hakatia helps Iakoub to identify the doors and the closet, to locate on the walls some photo montages that Dojna made, which he has asked to keep near him.

Then they all meet in the living room. The living room is a large, pleasant space with contemporary furniture. The sliding windows are wide open. The weather is hot. Hakatia tries to welcome her guests without any darkness in her voice or her manner. She has planned to behave naturally, as if she were with two old friends unimpeded by convention, who are free to walk here and there, to sit, to get up, free from all constraint. She sits in a corner with a cup of tea and a book, Iakoub Khadjbakiro's first novel. After a moment, Iakoub comes out of his room and moves toward the sofa. He advances carefully, making an effort to hide how he must find his way around the furniture with his fingertips. He sits, mute and meditative, with his face turned toward one of Dojna's paintings, a beautiful painting that he knows by heart. He does his best to reconstitute it, flame by flame, detail by detail, brushstroke by brushstroke. Perhaps he succeeds in this endeavor. From time to time he presses his lips to a teacup that Hakatia has placed before him. The porcelain clinks, the saucer, the small spoon. His hands tremble, robbed of their strength.

Later, Dimirtchi Makionian appears. He gives the impression of being fairly comfortable. He serves himself tea, sinks into a soft armchair in the sunshine. He drinks without hurrying, breathing in the steam that wavers on the liquid's surface. All three remain this way, calm, in almost opposite ends of the room. They do not force themselves to produce an artificial conversation. Then Dimirtchi Makionian rises, letting out a weak gasp when he stiffens his arm against the armrest. Hakatia inquires with her eyes, and he reassures her with a smile. He goes to shuffle through the collection of records lined up on her shelves. Hakatia Badrinourbat is a geologist and her areas of interest are mostly scientific, but she likes music and owns numerous recordings of classic and contemporary works. Dimirtchi Makionian's left arm hangs inert at his side, but he passes his mutilated right hand along the record covers. His manner is very casual. He examines the titles on the cardboard sleeves in which the records are preserved, sheltered from dust. He shows no sign of any particular agitation; without haste, he seeks whatever interests him. Then he pulls a black disk out of its translucent envelope. He places it on the turntable and starts the record player. The sound is pure, without a crackle. Dimirtchi Makionian has chosen, for this final scene, Naïsso Baldakchan's poem, a transcription for solo viola. The other side of the record holds Baldakchan's third quartet, but on this side, Tchaki Estherkhan plays without accompaniment.

As the poem rolls through its poignant, sweeping phrases, Dimirtchi Makionian turns away and moves, as if on tiptoe, to the window. He turns away from the other listeners, from the writer, from the geologist. This is the story of a cellist who turns away.

He looks out the window. Actually it's not a window, but the opening of a cavern, where birds live. Outside everything is steep, everything is blue: blue clouds, blue sun, blue abyss. When he leans out, he can see volcanoes, lakes, lava flows, mountains crowned in azure snow. The breeze is light, warm, full of perfume. He leans a little farther over the edge of the precipice. Expanses of grass shimmer, birds soar across the sky, feathers quivering. Some of them are not his kind, but that doesn't matter. He knows that, despite his injured wing, he will be able to fly. He listens to the music. He listens to Tchaki Estherkhan's viola that sings all around him, and when he takes off, he sees her.

ANTOINE VOLODINE (a heteronym) has written popular French novels under a variety of heteronyms, including Lutz Bassmann, Elli Kronauer, and Manuela Draeger. Several of his books have been recently translated: *Minor Angels*, *Radiant Terminus*, *Bardo or Not Bardo*, and *Writers*.

LIA SWOPE MITCHELL is a writer and translator from Minneapolis. Her short fiction has been published in the magazines *Asimov's*, *Apex*, *Shimmer*, and *Cosmos*. She is the translator of Georges Didi-Huberman's *Survival of the Fireflies* (Minnesota, 2018).